The Elphite

Michelle Gordon

www.theamethystangel.com

First published in Great Britain in 2012 by The Amethyst Angel
Second Edition Published in 2014 by The Amethyst Angel

Copyright © 2014 Michelle Gordon
Cover Design by madappledesigns copyright © madappledesigns

The moral right of the author has been asserted.

ISBN: 978-1499605594

Second Edition

Acknowledgements

A huge thank you to all of my readers who have sent me lovely e-mails and messages telling me how much they've enjoyed my books, and how my books have helped them in some way. It is these words that keep me writing, and remind me that all of the hard work is worth it. Thank you to all of you.

Thank you to all of my readers, editors and proof-readers: Elizabeth Lockwood, Laura Wilce, Alex Watts, Victor Keegan, Liz Gordon, Rachael Barnwell, Kimberley Denz, and Sally Byrne. Your comments and advice were very much appreciated, and the book is so much better for them.

Elizabeth Lockwood, you are a beautiful Angel and you have helped me so much, this book would never have happened without you. Thank you.

Thank you, Mum, for your continued support and belief in me. I love you more than you know!

Liz, you've inspired and supported me, and I appreciate all of your help so much, thank you. The cover is beautiful, so very thankful for your creative input.

Thank you, Jon. You have been my muse these past two years. You believed in me so much, that you have inspired me believe in myself, which is the most amazing thing anyone can do for another. You are so awesome, I love you.

Thank you to the following people, for their encouragement and love: Dad, Annette Ecuyere, Auntie Helen, Niki, Sarah & Alex, and all of the amazing people I have met through 4Networking,

Thank you Camp Nanowrimo! Without you I wouldn't have had the motivation to get the words out, and to keep writing. Thank you to Victor, who went on the camping trip with me!

Links

Elizabeth Lockwood
www.elizabethlockwood.co.uk

Liz Gordon
www.madappledesigns.co.uk

Laura Wilce and Alex Watts
www.luminousediting.com

Camp Nanowrimo
www.campnanowrimo.org

Victor Keegan
www.victorkeegan.com/

Rachael Barnwell
roomintheloft.wordpress.com/

This book is dedicated to my amazing family -

Mum, Dad, Liz, Andrew, Nanny, Auntie Helen, Ffion,
Annette & John.
Your support, encouragement and belief means the world to me.
Thank you for your love.

Prologue

My name is Ellie Smith, and I was born on the twenty-fifth of September, 1982. I know that's a very ordinary way to begin a story, but my story is anything but ordinary.

In fact, you may read it and not believe a word of it, but I assure you, everything is true. I remember everything that has ever happened, which as you will see, is not always a good thing.

Part One

Chapter One

He'd only just made it in time.

Breathing heavily, he slumped into the first empty seat he came to and tried to relax. So far his holiday had been one stressful event after another.

First, he'd forgotten his passport and had to speed home to retrieve it. Then, with only minutes to spare before the flight check-in closed, he'd been stung for having too much weight in his suitcase. Not having enough time to deal with it, he'd paid the extra, though now the dent in his wallet meant less spending money when he finally got to Spain. He'd sprinted to the boarding gate, made it onto the plane, and then found himself sitting next to a lady who smelled like she'd spent the last twenty years locked in a house full of cats.

After holding his breath for nearly two hours, the plane had finally touched down, and he'd got to the luggage area, only to find that the airline had lost his suitcase. They said it may turn up, in which case they'd send it to his hotel in a few days, but that meant until then, he had nothing to wear but the clothes on his back.

At least he'd made it onto the train from the airport. Of course, it had cost him an extra thirty-five euros to get the train from the airport in Zaragoza to his hotel in Barcelona. So much for taking it easy and having a break from his normally stressful life. He was beginning to wish he hadn't gone for the last-minute deal and had stayed somewhere closer to home instead. He sighed. At least he was only a few hours away from his destination now.

Breathing a little easier, Luke opened his eyes and sat up straight. He grabbed the rucksack at his feet and started to rummage through it, looking for the thriller that he'd brought with him. A sigh and a movement out of the corner of his eye made him look up.

The girl sat across from him met his gaze for a second, then quickly looked away. He tried to look down and concentrate on finding the novel, but he found he couldn't wrench his gaze away from her face. She sighed again and looked at him, holding his gaze for a fraction longer this time. When she looked away the second time, Luke began to wonder what was wrong with him. He tried several times to look away, but he couldn't do it for more than a few seconds. Not wanting her to turn her disapproving gaze on him for a third time, he abandoned his search and settled back in his seat, closing his eyes. But not completely. Through tiny slits, he continued to watch the girl as she pointedly stared out of the window.

She was beautiful. Perhaps not in a conventional sense; she certainly wasn't dressed to impress. But it wasn't her appearance that had him hooked. There was something about her that drew him in, almost forcing him to look at her. He shifted about in his seat, trying to get comfortable in his fake sleeping position. He saw the girl flick a glance at him, then look down at her bag, then look around the crowded train. Luke's heart constricted as he realised that she seemed to be deciding whether to stay sitting there or to find somewhere else. Bizarrely, considering he didn't know her name and had never heard her voice, Luke knew he couldn't bear for her to get up and leave now. What if he never saw her again?

He took in a deep, slow breath, opened his eyes and forced himself to stare out of the window. It helped that the reflection of the window meant that he could still see her. Tiny changes in her facial expression gave Luke the impression that she was having a pretty intense internal monologue. He wondered what she was thinking and why she had looked at him the way she had. Maybe she was just sick of strange men chatting her up and was trying to deter him. Or maybe she felt attracted to him but had a boyfriend, or even a husband.

Luke's gaze flicked down to her left hand. No ring, but that didn't mean she was definitely single. He moved his gaze back to her reflection, only lingering for a moment on her tanned, smooth, bare leg.

The girl frowned, closed her eyes and shook her head, causing Luke to wonder again what she was thinking. He tried to come up with an interesting opening to a conversation. Something that wouldn't make her feel awkward or send her running away screaming, or worse still - make her fall asleep. He'd never been very good at chatting up girls; he was normally far too shy. In his very few past relationships, the girls had usually chatted him up. Of course, once they got to know him and he'd relaxed, it was difficult to shut him up, especially when he got onto his favourite subjects. Luke yawned suddenly and blinked. *Come on*, he told himself. *Focus on the matter at hand, what do I say to her?*

He saw her hand clutch at her bag a little tighter and she glanced at her watch. Luke knew that if he didn't say something in the next thirty seconds, she might move on. Gathering all the courage he had, he swallowed hard and then spoke.

"So have you been to Barcelona before?"

His voice sounded weird to his own ears, and his stupid

question echoed all around him as people glanced at him to see who he was speaking to. He watched the girl openly now, hoping that she would answer and not make him feel any more ridiculous than he already felt. She looked at him, her gaze piercing. He noticed now that she had bright blue eyes, with tiny flecks of grey running through them.

In a controlled, almost hostile voice, she answered. "Yes, thank you."

Luke blinked, confused by her tone. Her accent was too subtle to pick out where she was from. She could have been English, but then she could have been American or Canadian, too.

"Do you like it there? I've never been there before." Grimacing internally at his banal questions, Luke waited for her response, hoping for more this time.

She appeared to be struggling with something when she replied. "It's okay. I prefer Paris."

Definitely American, probably East Coast, Luke decided. Maybe she was just being hostile because she was American; he'd heard that they could be quite rude to people when they were travelling.

"Why aren't you in Paris then?" he joked, badly.

He saw her mutter something under her breath. He wasn't sure, but it looked like 'I wish I was'. Luke frowned. American or not, there really was no need for her rudeness. He considered shutting up and actually going to sleep. But something compelled him to ignore his wounded ego - and the humiliation of the other passengers watching him completely bomb - and continue.

"I've never been to Paris, maybe I'll go there on my next holiday. I only chose Barcelona because the deal was cheap and it was leaving at the right time. Though, after all the problems I've had getting here, it's not turned out to be very cheap, after all."

The girl nodded without commenting. Luke thought she looked like she was wondering why the hell he was still trying to talk to her. Why was he? It made no sense, not even to himself. He'd never felt like this before. He wondered idly if he was being possessed by something.

"Make sure you go in the spring, to Paris. It's beautiful then."

Luke smiled at the lady with the Australian accent sat next to him, hoping that she wouldn't take it as an invitation to keep talking.

"My husband took me there for our tenth anniversary in April and it was wonderful. Wasn't too hot either, at that time of year. Just the right temperature I think, no need for heavy clothes, but you don't melt either. We were going to go up the Eiffel Tower, but my husband is afraid of heights and I didn't want to go up by myself, what would be the point in that? Maybe I'll go back one day with..."

Luke turned from the Australian lady, trying to tune her out. The girl looked like she was trying not to smile; she even looked a little bit smug that she'd been let off the hook by the kind lady who wouldn't shut up. She was now going on about the French bread and how they'd had a perfect picnic in the park by the Louvre.

How could he try and strike up a conversation with the girl now? Luke wished he'd been raised to be a little less polite, then he would have told the Australian to shut up while he tried to talk to the girl. However, he was doing such a terrible job of it, maybe she was just saving him the further embarrassment of being snubbed again.

Another passenger across the carriage decided to join in the conversation, asking a question about Paris, so the Australian lady moved to a seat closer to her. Soon they were chatting away, ignoring Luke completely. Luke was relieved. He only had an hour and a half left of his journey to try and connect with the girl. First things first, he really wanted to know her name.

He decided to go for the direct approach.

"My name's Luke."

The girl raised an eyebrow, as if to say 'lucky you', but said nothing.

Luke wanted to kick something in frustration. Why was she being so aloof? Would it really kill her to be polite and reciprocate?

"Are you on holiday? Whereabouts in America are you from?" There. She couldn't possibly avoid direct questions like that without being unbelievably rude. Though so far, it didn't seem like she cared what other people thought of her.

"No, I'm not on holiday. And no, I'm not American, either."

Luke waited for her to elaborate, but apparently she wasn't going to. Just then, an announcement cut through the tense silence, naming the next station stop. With the slightest nod of her head to Luke, the girl all but jumped out of her seat and left the carriage as soon as the train rolled to a stop. Luke watched her slim form race down the platform to the exit. He swore under his breath.

After a few moments of indecision, he leapt up, ignored the looks he received from the other passengers, and stepped through the doors a second before they closed. Now what? He had no choice but to run. He slung the rucksack on his back, suddenly glad that his suitcase had been lost, because he would never have been able to pursue the girl if he'd had it with him.

His feet flew down the platform and he made his way out of the station, doing his best not to flatten anyone in the process. He stopped for a second outside and scanned the street in front of him. A flurry of movement at the end of the street caught his attention and before he'd fully processed it, he was off again. His rucksack thumped against his back, making his shirt stick to the sweat running down it. The Spanish sun that he'd been looking forward to now just seemed cruel.

He reached the end of the street and turned the corner. He skidded to a stop and stepped back. The girl was just a few metres away, leaning into the open window of a taxi. She glanced around her, then opened the passenger door and jumped in.

The taxi sped off, giving Luke only seconds to leap out into the road, frantically trying to flag a taxi, or in fact, anyone, down. He couldn't lose her now. Moments later, another taxi came into sight and Luke threw himself into the back of it, shouting for the taxi driver to follow the taxi in front.

Luckily, the driver must have been a film fan and understood him, because he put his foot down and within a minute, they were just a couple of cars behind. Luke gripped onto the headrest of the front passenger seat, his eyes glued on the taxi in front. His heart was thumping, and he briefly wondered why he was acting like an insane man, but then decided that it didn't matter. He felt more alive chasing after this girl than he had felt in his entire life. Screw logical and sensible - what he was doing was utterly crazy, but it felt completely right.

He barely noticed the buildings they passed as the taxi sped down the sometimes scarily narrow streets. At least the driver seemed to be having a good time. Luke's insane actions had brightened up at least one person's day.

The taxi came to a stop suddenly and Luke saw the girl get out of the taxi up ahead.

"How much?" he asked the driver frantically, scrabbling for his wallet in his back pocket. Without waiting to hear the reply, Luke pulled out a wad of euros and threw them onto the front seat. He jumped out of the taxi and hurried up the narrow path, trying to keep the girl in his sights. He lost her briefly as she turned a corner, so he started to jog. When he reached the corner, however, he slowed to a walk, which was good, because otherwise he would have ploughed into her and knocked her over.

She glared at him with unabashed annoyance as he fought to slow his heartbeat down.

"Are you following me?"

He opened his mouth to explain, but found that there really was no acceptable explanation. After floundering for a few moments, he said the only thing he could think of.

"I'm sorry."

She raised her eyebrows and then sighed. "Wasn't I clear enough on the train? I don't want to speak to you."

Luke frowned. "Why not?"

She shrugged. "I just don't, okay? Now please leave me alone." She turned to leave but Luke reached out and grabbed her.

When his hand touched her bare arm, the familiarity of her soft skin made his fingers tingle. Shocked, he held on tightly, not wanting to let her leave. She looked down at his hand, and again, a million unspoken thoughts and emotions played across her face.

"What do you want from me?" she whispered.

Luke shook his head. "I don't know. I'm sorry, I'm not normally this crazy, I promise. I just felt like I *needed* to speak to you. Please tell me your name."

The girl smiled, but it didn't reach her eyes. "Please just let me go. It's for the best, trust me."

Luke shook his head again, refusing to loosen his grip on her arm. "Just tell me your name, please."

The girl met his eyes and smiled her half smile again. "I

will tell you my name if you let me go and promise not to follow me any further."

Luke nodded quickly and reluctantly let go of her arm, regretting the red mark that he left behind.

"My name is Ellie. Goodbye, Luke." With that, she ran down the street, disappearing into a building, leaving Luke staring after her, a feeling of sorrow lodged in his chest where his heart used to be.

*   *   *

Not again.

How had it happened? Ellie thought she'd done everything possible to avoid him, yet somehow he had managed to find her again. It was just crazy. What were the chances of him being on the same train, at the same time, in Spain, of all places? Maybe she should have just erred on the side of caution and stayed away from trains for the entire year. Then she'd probably have ended up meeting him on a plane or something. And to think she'd purposely moved to another country to avoid this situation happening again.

She leaned against the wooden door-frame and groaned. Perhaps she should have just hibernated for the year, then there would have been no chance of their paths crossing, would there?

Shaking her head at herself, she moved slowly down the hallway to the lounge, dumping her satchel on the sofa.

Her cat, Mañana, came to greet her; hungry, no doubt. Ellie went into the kitchen and began her normal evening routine. Feed the cat, make dinner, sit on the terrace and enjoy the sunshine. Okay, so moving to Spain definitely had its benefits. Ellie wished she had done it before, even if it hadn't really helped her when it came to Luke. Perhaps she should have moved to an island in the middle of the Pacific. Knowing her luck though, he would have found her there, too.

Her internal musings were interrupted by the peal of the doorbell. She froze in place and closed her eyes. *Please go away. Please.*

The doorbell went again. Her unspoken pleas turned into muttered expletives.

She gave it a few more minutes, but when it rang a third time, she knew that he wasn't going to give up. She looked around the lounge and wished it was a bit messier; it would have helped.

She walked as slowly as possible to the front door, dragging her bare feet across the cool tiles. She turned the key and pulled the door open slightly. She looked out and saw Luke's back as he paced up and down the path. He spun around at the sound of the creaking hinges.

"Look, before you say anything, I know I said I would leave you alone, but the truth is: I can't. I wish I knew why I'm acting like this, but I don't. I don't want to scare you, or annoy you; I just really want to talk to you, Ellie."

Ellie sighed. She opened the door a little wider and her shoulders slumped in defeat. "You'd better come in then."

Luke's eyes widened and she saw that she'd surprised him. He was probably expecting more resistance. Damn. Maybe she could have pushed him away if she'd tried a little harder. Too late now.

She stepped aside and waved him in, noticing with amusement how he almost ran up the steps. She closed the door and followed him into the lounge. Luke was stood in the middle, hands in his pockets, looking awkward.

"Would you like something to drink?"

He smiled at her. "Yes, please." He pulled the rucksack off his back and placed it on the settee.

Ellie went into the kitchen to make the drinks, gesturing for him to follow her. Out on the terrace, they settled onto the loungers and she silently sipped her drink while she tried to figure out what to say to him. She'd never been at a loss for words around him before, but this time was different. This time, she wanted to change things, but her plans were already in ruins. She needed a new plan, and fast.

"Thank you for not calling the police. Following you like that was, well, the weirdest thing I've ever done, and I'm sorry if I scared you. I just wanted, well, actually, I just *needed* to talk to you."

Ellie sat up a little and smiled at him. "Don't worry, you didn't scare me, Luke. I don't scare that easily."

Luke smiled back, relief radiating from him. He sat up as well, leaning toward Ellie as he spoke again.

"You're being rather calm about a complete stranger following you to your home, then getting himself invited in for a drink. Is this a regular thing for you?"

Ellie laughed then, the sound echoed off the low white walls of the terrace. She shook her head. "No, this isn't a regular thing. It's complicated to explain why I feel safe with you, Luke."

Luke frowned. "Please try to explain."

Ellie sighed, her smile slipping away. "It's never been like this before. I've never explained it before. I've just, well, pretended. But I'm tired of pretending, it never changes anything in the end. It doesn't matter what I do, or how I do it or when I do it," Ellie jumped up, her agitation causing her to pace the tiny terrace. "I don't understand. This time, I was sure that if I changed us, that if we didn't meet, it would be enough to change everything. But here you are again!" She flung her arm out at him, almost accusingly. "And here we go, again. It's never going to end, is it?"

She stopped her frantic pacing and stared down at him, her hands on her hips.

Luke looked up at her in confusion. "I have absolutely no idea what you're on about. But it sounds like," he stood up and took a hesitant step toward her, "we've met before?"

Ellie sighed. "Yes. More than once."

Luke reached for her, and as his hand touched her bare skin again, the electric current between them was undeniable.

"That would explain why I feel so drawn to you," Luke murmured. "But if we've met before, how come I don't remember?"

Ellie closed the gap between them and laid her head on his chest. She felt him wrap his arms around her and rest his chin on the top of her head. How could she possibly have avoided this? Why would she want to, when it felt so good?

"I don't know where to start," she whispered.

Luke tightened his hold on her. "The beginning is always a good place."

Ellie chuckled. "That's the problem, there is no beginning. There is no end either; it's just one continuous loop."

There was silence then, punctuated only by a bird in a nearby tree and the sounds of cars passing the front of the house.

"Perhaps we should have another drink first. I get the feeling that this is going to be a very long and complicated explanation."

Ellie laughed again and pulled back a little. "I'll get the drinks. Would you like a shower, too?"

Luke raised an eyebrow. "Do I smell that bad?"

Ellie bit her lip. "Um, no, I just thought, you know, sometimes it's nice to freshen up after travelling."

Luke smiled at her blatant lie. "Okay, that would be good, actually. Though I'm afraid the airline lost my luggage, so I don't have any spare clothes."

"Not a problem. I have some clothes upstairs that an old room-mate left behind. They should fit you."

"In that case, lead the way."

Chapter Two

Luke took his time in the shower, but was too lost in his thoughts to really notice the hot water streaming down his body. The events of the last few hours were just too weird for him to comprehend. One minute he was just an ordinary guy, having terrible luck with his holiday. The next minute, he had been thrown into another world, where he felt this incredible love and attachment to a complete stranger that he barely knew.

Following her was so out of character for him. If any of his work colleagues could see him now, they wouldn't recognise him. Then there was Ellie's explanation, or lack of explanation, actually. They'd met before? When? How? Where? Why couldn't he remember? Was this real? Or was it just some scam or scheme to reel him in and rob him?

He shook his head at his thoughts. There was no way she was trying to rob him. She couldn't possibly have created the feelings inside him right now. They were definitely real.

He shut off the water and stepped out of the shower. He grabbed the towel she'd set out for him and rubbed himself dry quickly. Since the moment he'd set eyes on Ellie, his entire world had changed. It actually pained him now to be away from her for more than a few minutes. He shook his head again. If only his ex-girlfriends could see him now. They'd all complained about his lack of commitment and his inability to show emotion and his feelings for them. They wouldn't recognise him right now either.

After slipping on the clothes she'd found for him, Luke wiped the steam from the mirror with the towel and looked at his reflection. Though it hardly seemed possible, even he didn't recognise the face that stared back at him. How could everything change so drastically within a few short hours?

Luke folded the towel and put it on the side of the bath. After making sure he left everything as neat as possible, he then made his way back downstairs.

As he walked through the lounge, he saw Ellie through the window, out on the terrace, she seemed to be looking though a book. He went through the kitchen, grabbed the pitcher of lemonade on his way, and joined her outside.

Ellie looked up when she heard him. She closed the book and tucked it underneath her lounger.

"Feel better?"

Luke nodded and settled onto the other lounger. "Much, thanks." Luke poured them both a glass and they drank in silence for a few minutes.

"You would think that after all this time, I would have found a way to explain this… situation to people. But I haven't found a good way yet."

"You've told people about it before? Have you told me before?"

"I've told more people than I care to remember, but no, I've never told you."

"Why don't you just start wherever you want, and I'll do my best to keep up?"

Ellie smiled and nodded. She took a deep breath. "Do you know anything about the concept of reincarnation?"

Luke raised his eyebrows. "Well, I don't know the ins

and outs, but yeah, I know the general theory."

"That's good. It's a lovely concept and I wish more than anything it was true, but it's not. It's wrong. There is in fact a completely different reality."

"Okay," Luke said slowly, wondering what on earth she meant. How could she know that reincarnation didn't really exist?

"The idea that we have many different lives, learning different lessons in each, our souls evolving each time, is not accurate. We do in fact live several lifetimes. But not as different people."

Luke held up a hand. "Sorry, I think you may have lost me already."

Ellie smiled. "I told you I had no idea how to explain this. Basically, when we die, we don't go to heaven, hell, the other side or wherever, and then get reborn into a new body and live a new life. When we die, we are immediately reborn, as the same person."

"The same person? What do you mean?"

"You were born on September twelfth, 1982, right?"

"Uh, yeah, I was," Luke replied, surprised for a moment, before remembering that they had supposedly met before, so of course she would know that.

"When you die, you will be immediately reborn, as Luke Neil Whitchurch on September twelfth in 1982."

Luke frowned as he took in the meaning of her words. "Are you saying that we just live the same life over and over?"

Ellie smiled sadly. "Yep. It's like Groundhog Day, the film, only it lasts for a lifetime."

"Hang on though, why doesn't anyone know this? How do *you* know this?"

"Because no one remembers. That's the whole point: no one is supposed to remember."

"But you do?"

"Yes, I do. I wish I didn't, but I remember every single lifetime."

Luke looked even more puzzled. "But why?"

Ellie laughed and shook her head. "Don't you think I've spent every one of my lifetimes trying to figure that out?" She stood up and began to pace again. "Believe me, I wish I didn't. I wish I was completely unaware, like the rest of the world. Do you even realise how lucky you are? Living each life with no previous memories? You get to see the world the way a child does, with new eyes. You get to make decisions and have experiences with no recollection of the many times you've lived them before. But me? I just get to do the same damn thing over and over again."

Luke watched her pace up and down the small terrace, unsure of what to say. "You mean you don't change anything? You don't do things differently each time?"

"Of course I try to change things! You wouldn't believe the number of disasters, accidents, meetings and deaths I have tried to prevent or change. But it doesn't matter what I do, the outcome is always the same. I mean take you, for example," she said, pointing at him accusingly. "We have met in every lifetime, and our relationship has been pretty much the same in every one of them. But this time, I thought that maybe if we didn't meet, I could change the ending. I could finally change my fate. So I moved to Spain. I moved to this tiny remote village, thinking I couldn't possibly meet you now, and here you are! On bloody schedule too! Which means that yet again, we are headed for the same fate as always. I don't know why I bother!"

She sank down on the lounger, the life seemingly drained from her.

Luke was at a loss. He'd never heard of such a thing

before. The idea that he had spent many lifetimes in love with this beautiful woman amazed him, yet made perfect sense at the same time. He'd never felt so attracted to another person before.

Ellie was silent for a long time, and Luke watched the shadows of the evening move across her face. He shifted awkwardly in his seat and drank the last of his lemonade. Just as he was about to say something, she spoke.

"You must think I'm completely crazy."

Luke smiled at her, reaching across the space between them, to take her hand in his. "No, I don't think you're crazy. I'm not really sure what to think, to be honest."

Ellie squeezed his hand and nodded. "I don't expect you to know what to think. Over the last few lifetimes I've spoken to all kinds of people: spiritualists, priests, scientists, even doctors, and none of them knew what to make of it either."

"How many lifetimes have you spent locked up in asylums then?" Luke kidded.

Ellie chuckled darkly. "Only one. Then I wised up to the fact I should never speak to a psychologist."

Luke's eyebrows shot up. "How did we have a relationship in that life?"

Ellie smiled. "We didn't meet until after I was released. Took a hell of a lot of lying to get myself out of that one."

Luke's eyebrows lowered a fraction, but he said nothing. It all seemed a little too Sci-Fi to be true. "Did I know about that? In that lifetime?"

"That I was a certified nutter? No, of course not."

"Wow, and here I was thinking that relationships were supposed to be based on honesty and trust."

Ellie laughed again. "I'm afraid the world isn't really the place you think it is."

"Apparently not," Luke agreed dryly. "So, none of these

so-called experts knew what to make of this?"

"No, none of them had ever come across the idea. I've been labelled as everything from delusional to highly imaginative to a wise sage. Obviously," she added when he laughed, "I'm none of those things. I'm not some kind of superhero. I'm just an ordinary person attempting to live my life, with the unfortunate bonus that I get to do it over and over again."

"So we've been together in every one of those lives?" Luke asked, still trying to make sense of it all.

"Yes, every one."

Luke remembered her earlier ranting. "And that's a bad thing? Why didn't you want to meet me this time?"

Ellie frowned. "I was trying to change things. In every life, I've changed everything I can think of, except for meeting you. I figured if I changed that, then maybe I could change the ending."

"I thought you said it never ended? It's just a continuous loop?"

"I'd forgotten how nit-picky you are," Ellie commented, rolling her eyes. "I meant I was trying to change the end of my life, the part where I die."

Luke took a deep breath. "And you thought that if you didn't meet me, you wouldn't die? You wouldn't have to go through the cycle again so quickly? Do I cause your death?" Overcome with sorrow at the idea of losing her, at the idea of being the cause of her demise, Luke leaned over to her and gripped her hands.

Ellie sighed. "I think I now know why I never explained this before. It was much easier when you were oblivious. No, Luke, you aren't the cause of my death."

"What happens then? Why didn't you want to meet me?"

Ellie raised her eyes to meet Luke's. Her exhausted

expression stopped him from uttering another question. Suddenly, he felt completely exhausted himself.

"Maybe we should just take a break from all this for a bit. I think I need some time to digest it all."

Ellie nodded gratefully. She lay back on the lounger and closed her eyes.

Luke released her hands and lay back on his own lounger, staring up at the stars that had appeared. His mind was racing with everything he had discovered in the last few hours. His whole world had changed so dramatically that he couldn't quite believe he had woken up as normal in his own bed just that morning. Could Ellie be telling the truth?

He glanced over at her, noticing that her expression had relaxed, and her breathing had slowed. She had no reason to lie to him. After all, he was a stranger, someone that she had met randomly on a train.

But she didn't feel like a stranger to him. He felt like he'd known her forever. And according to her theory, he had.

Next to him, Ellie shivered in her sleep. Luke swung his legs round and stood up. As carefully as he could, he lifted Ellie up and carried her upstairs. She barely stirred in his arms as he set her down on the bed and tucked her underneath the white sheets. He smoothed a stray lock of hair from her face and then left the room.

Back on the terrace, Luke poured himself a vodka, having found a bottle tucked away under the sink. His brain felt completely fried, but he knew he wouldn't be able to fall asleep without a little help.

Chapter Three

Ellie awoke with a start the next day. She sat up and realised that she was fully clothed in bed. She remembered the events of the previous day and simultaneously smiled and groaned. She couldn't even begin to imagine how many questions he would have for her today.

Throwing off the covers, she leapt off the bed and stretched. The sun was shining through the window, making Ellie glad that she had chosen somewhere warm for her hiding place.

Wrapping herself in her dressing gown, she tiptoed barefoot to the spare room and peeked in through the open door. The room was exactly as it had been yesterday, the bed hadn't been touched. Frowning, Ellie made her way a little more quickly down the stairs to the ground floor. A glance around the room made her heart speed up. Had he left? Had it all been too weird for him last night?

She went into the kitchen and a movement out on the terrace caught her eye. She went out the sliding door and smiled at Luke's curled-up form on the lounger. She saw the vodka bottle on the ground next to him and rolled her eyes. It seemed his habits hadn't changed. Apparently his snoring hadn't improved, either. Ellie sighed. Despite everything, she really couldn't imagine being with anyone else. Probably because she never had been.

She stared at him a little longer, then went back into the kitchen and started making some pancakes. She put the kettle on the stove to make some tea, and hummed a tune to herself.

"Morning, sleepy head," Ellie sang as she walked back out onto the terrace, a steaming cup of tea and plate of pancakes in hand.

Luke sat up suddenly, then grabbed his head and groaned.

"Regretting the little vodka binge?"

Luke looked up at her and blinked rapidly. "So it wasn't a dream?"

Ellie smiled and sat on the lounger next to him. She handed him the tea and pancakes. "I'm afraid not. You really did stalk a total stranger, follow her to her home, find out that she's a total nutcase, then drink her emergency alcohol and pass out on a sun lounger."

Luke sipped the hot tea then set it on the table. "You're not a total nutter. At least, I don't think you are."

Ellie laughed. "That's good to know." She gestured for him to eat and he tucked into the pancakes with enthusiasm. "I bet you have all sorts of questions for me, don't you?"

Luke swallowed his mouthful and frowned. "I guess. Though they're probably not very good questions."

"Don't worry, I'm not grading you, and as this is a fairly crazy situation, there are no stupid questions, either."

Luke nodded slowly, trying to think, despite the vodka-induced fuzziness in his brain. "What's your last name?"

Ellie blinked in surprise. "That's an easy one. My last name is Smith."

"How old are you?"

"I'm twenty-two. Same as you."

Luke ate another mouthful of pancakes slowly, while

Ellie tried to anticipate his next question. She was surprised that he wanted to know such mundane details about her, rather than the more complex details about the way they had lived their lives repeatedly.

"Have you fallen out of love with me?"

Ellie's mouth opened and closed a few times. She had definitely not been expecting that. "I don't understand what you mean, we only met yesterday."

"We've lived many lives together already, none of which I remember, all of which you do remember. But this time, you were trying to avoid meeting me, so I wondered if it was because you didn't love me anymore, because you didn't want to be with me?"

Despite his matter of fact tone, Ellie knew Luke well enough to see the pain in his eyes and the fear in his expression. She knew that when he was just twelve years old, his mother had abandoned him. She'd run away to live with someone she'd met on holiday. Feeling unfamiliar tears beginning to gather, Ellie reached out and laid her hand on his. She realised that she had been selfish in her bid to avoid her fate, and she regretted the hurt she had now caused.

She caught his gaze and held it. "I love you, Luke. I have always loved you. From the very first time we met, until right now. I don't think there will be a single second of my many lives that I won't be in love with you."

Luke stared back, a smile tugging at his lips. "Really?"

Ellie smiled. "Truly." She squeezed his hand. "And if my attempt to avoid you had been successful, I'm quite certain that I would have been completely miserable for the rest of my short life."

Luke's eyes narrowed at her choice of words. "Short?"

Ellie sighed again. She kept forgetting how good he was at picking out the details. She waved her hand in an attempt to brush it off. "Figure of speech. Didn't mean anything by it."

Luke frowned again but accepted her word. At least he was still as trusting as always. He dug into his remaining pancakes and gulped down the now cool tea.

Ellie lay back on the lounger, still feeling a little sleepy despite her deep sleep the night before. She closed her eyes and waited for his next question.

"So what happens then?"

Ellie opened one eye and peered sideways at Luke, who was finishing his tea. "What do you mean? What happens?"

"In our lives. What we do, what we don't do, how it ends."

Ellie frowned. "Why would you want to know any of that? It would drive you crazy, knowing exactly what's going to happen in your life."

Luke raised an eyebrow. "You're not crazy."

"That's because I'm used to it. But believe me, it took several lives for me to get used to it. And it wasn't easy." She sighed. "Now, every day, I wake up wishing that I didn't know what was going to happen. That I didn't know how it was all going to end. I would rather live my life in complete uncertainty, never knowing what's going to happen next. Where I'm going to go, who I'm going to meet. But that's never going to happen for me." Ellie looked at Luke, who had stopped eating and was now staring at her.

"You should enjoy that. It's one of the best parts about living. The uncertainty."

Luke frowned. "I don't know. I think I could do with a little certainty in my life."

"Really? You would want to know the dates for when things were going to happen in your life? You would want to know when you were going to lose your friends and your family? You would want to know when there's going to be a national disaster and thousands of people are going to be killed – all the while knowing that there's absolutely nothing you can do about it? You would want that?"

"No, well, when you put it that way, I guess I wouldn't." Luke finished his pancakes and set the plate on the table. "So what should I ask you, if I can't ask you about our lives?"

Ellie shrugged. "I don't know. Like I said yesterday, I've never told you all of this before. And I've never told anyone who believed me before, either. So this is actually a new experience for me."

Luke smiled. "So that's a good thing, right? It's not the same thing again, something has actually changed?"

Ellie smiled back. "I guess so, yeah. Though I don't think that you knowing will make that much difference to our lives and the outcome, ultimately."

"How do you know? Perhaps this is the change that changes everything."

Ellie reached across the gap between them and took his hand. She squeezed it softly. "Maybe. I guess I've just stopped hoping."

Luke leaned forward and touched her cheek. "Tell me what to do to make things better."

"I'd forgotten how much you love to fix things." She shook her head. "I don't think there's anything you can do to fix this situation. We're all just doomed to live the same life on repeat. In the next lifetime, you won't remember that any of this happened. Next time, I promise I will just let things happen the way they always do with us. I won't tell you everything, then you can just live in blissful ignorance again."

Luke shook his head. "No, I wouldn't want that. I'm

glad that you've told me. Because now, together, we can change things. It doesn't have to be like last time, or the time before."

"Or the time before that? How are you proposing to make things different then?" Ellie pulled her hand away from Luke's, picked up the china and went inside to the kitchen. She set the plate and cup in the sink and looked through the window at Luke's profile. She hated to be so negative when he was trying to make things right, but she just couldn't see how he could make it any better. Despite him saying he was glad he knew the truth, Ellie was regretting telling him anything.

What good would it do? Instead of just driving her crazy, the knowledge would drive him crazy, too.

She saw him get up, and a few moments later, felt his body heat through her dressing gown. He laid a hand on her shoulder and she closed her eyes.

"Ellie?"

She loved the way he said her name. "What?"

"Do you trust me?"

Ellie smiled and turned to face him. "You know I do."

"Then trust me when I say that things will be different this time."

Ellie took a deep breath. "Okay." She closed her eyes a second before his lips met hers.

Chapter Four

Luke kissed Ellie gently on the lips, ready, this time, for the electric shock that came with touching her bare skin. Nothing had ever felt this right to him before. He felt like he had come home, that he belonged in her arms, his lips on hers.

He had no idea how he was going to make things different. Right now, all he wanted to do was to be with her, he couldn't think of anything else. He pulled back a little and looked down at her serene features.

"Ellie?"

She opened her eyes and looked up at him. "What?"

"What do you want to do?"

Ellie smiled. "I was quite enjoying kissing you, actually. Why?"

Luke chuckled. "No, I don't mean right now. I mean in life. What have you always wanted to do? If money was no object?"

"Why?"

"I just want to know."

Ellie shook her head. "I don't know. I suppose I would just like to not know what's going to happen next. What do you want to do?"

Luke smiled. "Travel around the world. See all of the cultures and countries that I've only ever seen on TV or in films."

Ellie laughed and shook her head.

"What? What's so funny?"

"I don't know why I asked you that. I knew what the answer would be. It's always been your answer to that question. Throughout all of our lives together, that's all you've ever wanted to do."

Luke frowned. "You're making me feel utterly predictable right now."

Ellie chuckled again. "Sorry. I can't help it, I know you better than you know yourself."

"So did we do it?"

Ellie raised an eyebrow. "Did we do what?"

"Travel around the world together?"

"No, of course not."

Luke took Ellie's hand and led her over to the settee. The cool of the lounge was preferable to the heat of the late morning sunshine. Once they were settled, he turned to her again.

"Why not?"

"Because we never had the money. We had jobs and I was trying to live a normal life. And besides, you only believe in doing things that you can afford to. You would never have agreed to go and pay for it with credit cards."

Luke frowned. She was right, of course. He'd never been in debt and avoided credit cards like the plague.

"We could have saved up, surely?"

Ellie shook her head. "We tried that. But each time, either there were expenses that ate our savings, or..." Ellie's voice trailed off then, and Luke frowned at her.

"Or?"

"Nothing. We tried. But it didn't work out. We did go on holidays though."

"Or what, Ellie? What were you going to say?" Luke could see by her expression that she regretted her words, but he needed to know why they hadn't followed their dreams before.

She shook her head. "I told you already, if you knew everything that was going to happen, it would drive you crazy."

Luke sighed. Though he was glad that she'd confided this much in him, it was going to kill him to know that there were still so many secrets that she was keeping.

Ellie stared up at him, and he could see her trying to read his expression. He leaned down to kiss her and she relaxed a little.

"Now that I do know what's happening, or at least some of it, there's no need for pretences anymore. So why don't we do it?"

Ellie frowned. "Do what?"

"Travel around the world. Change things. Make this life completely different to all of the ones that have gone before. I mean, I know that money *is* actually an object, and one that I don't have a whole lot of, but I'm sure we could find a way to do it. Maybe even use a few credit cards. We could start with Europe, then go further afield."

"Are you serious?"

"Absolutely. I know that you've lived it over and over, but it feels like the first time for me, and I want to do it right. So I think that we should do everything that we've never done before and live this life as if it's our last one together." Luke jumped up and started pacing up and down the rattan rug. "Let's make every moment count. I don't want to spend my days working in a boring job, wasting precious time that could be spent with you." He stopped pacing, and suddenly knelt down in front of Ellie. The events of the previous twenty-four hours had been the craziest of his life, but what he was about to do next was the craziest thing by far.

"Ellie Smith. Will you marry me?"

*   *   *

Ellie blinked in surprise. Well, this was certainly different. The Luke that she knew and loved would never do something so crazy and spontaneous.

"Luke, what are you doing?" she whispered.

"Do you mean I haven't done this before? I haven't proposed to you within a day of meeting you?"

Ellie shook her head. "No, you haven't. It's always taken you at least two years to ask me to marry you before."

"Two years! How on earth did I wait that long?"

"You've never been this spontaneous. Usually everything has to be meticulously planned and organised. Which is why I was surprised that you were on a last minute holiday to Barcelona. You never do anything at the last minute."

"Then maybe I've changed in this lifetime, too."

"You still drink too much and snore."

Luke laughed. "I don't know what I can do about the snoring, but I will cut down on the alcohol if it bothers you." Luke shifted a little. "So what do you say? It seems that we're destined to be together no matter what we do. So why not make it official right away?"

Ellie sighed. "Because now it just feels like we're doing this because we have no choice. Like we're just giving in to fate because it's pointless trying to fight it."

Luke frowned and finally got up from the floor and sat beside Ellie again. "So what should we do?"

Ellie bit her lip. "I don't know. I'm just too tired to think about it all. To try and figure out all the possibilities. Not that it'll change the end, anyway."

"If you mention the inevitable end once more, you're going to have to give me more details."

Ellie shook her head. "Believe me, you really don't want to know."

Luke sat back and closed his eyes. Then suddenly he sat up again, making Ellie jump.

"Okay, let's not plan anything mad today. Let's just do what a normal couple would do. Go out, eat food, see the sights, hold hands, etcetera. We should spend the day as if we don't know what's going to happen."

Ellie smiled and shrugged. "Okay, that's a lot tamer than running out to the nearest church and getting married. So, sure. Why not?"

Without further comment, Luke jumped up and started rummaging through his rucksack. He seemed to be back to his organised self again, Ellie noted. She got up and went upstairs to get ready.

*   *   *

Luke really couldn't believe how quickly things had changed. He had gone from living a boring, predictable life to living a spontaneous one with a woman he had apparently spent many lifetimes with. He looked down at Ellie, her face peaceful in sleep, and smiled. Despite a few premature stress lines on her face, she really was beautiful. He wondered if sleeping was the only escape she had from the heavy knowledge she possessed. He glanced at the clock; it was two in the morning and he just couldn't fall asleep.

Not wanting to disturb Ellie, he slid out from under the covers and crept out of the room. He went downstairs to see if there was any vodka left. He knew he'd promised to cut down his alcohol consumption, but he was used to having at least one drink before bed.

He went out to the terrace and was surprised to find that the night air was still pleasantly warm. He found the vodka bottle under the lounger and was pleased to see it still had some contents left. He sat on the lounger and tipped the bottle to his lips, enjoying the sting of the neat liquor on the back of his throat.

It had been a fantastic day. They hadn't done anything special, they had just done what any other couple would do on holiday, but it had been the best day of Luke's life. He'd felt so incredibly lucky to have Ellie on his arm; to hear her laughter and to find out more about her. It still freaked him out a little, just how much she knew about him, but he figured he'd get used to it.

He was still desperately curious about how it would all end, but at the same time, wasn't sure he was ready to know.

He sighed and looked down at the bottle in his hand. A rectangle of brown leather under the other lounger caught his eye.

Before he could stop himself, he leaned down and picked it up. It was an ordinary-looking diary, and its unremarkable cover did not in any way portray its incredible contents. Luke sat with it on his lap for several minutes, before he slugged down the rest of the vodka and turned to the first page.

Chapter Five

When Ellie opened her eyes to find herself alone in bed, she knew instantly that something was wrong. Before she had even fully awakened, she leapt out of bed and ran to the door, grabbing her dressing gown on the way. She didn't even bother checking the spare room, she just ran down the stairs to the lounge. Luke's rucksack was gone. She went out to the terrace and found what she had hoped she wouldn't.

An empty vodka bottle and her diary.

She sat down heavily on the lounger and squeezed her eyes shut. She'd never been this careless before. She never left her diary out for anyone to read. The contents were just too dangerous in the wrong hands. She flipped through the pages until she reached her last entry.

I hate Luke. I hate the fact that my life is so empty without him. I hate the fact that I love him so deeply, and I hate that when our lives intertwine, my fate is sealed. The only way I can change things is to not meet him, to make sure our paths do not cross. And if by some crazy synchronicity, they do cross, then the best I can hope to do is to make him hate me, and to get rid of him.

She rubbed her eyes. How could she have been so careless? Though she had written that just hours before they had met again, she no longer felt that way. She didn't believe that it was their relationship that brought about her death. Not anymore. Telling him the truth and having him share her burdens had made her feel lighter than she had felt in many lifetimes. And now that he knew, they could change things. They could make this life so different to all the others, that maybe it would be enough to change the ending. Perhaps they didn't have to be apart for her to live longer.

Ellie sighed. She wished he hadn't left without talking to her. She knew that she could find him if she wanted to, after all, she knew from previous lives where he lived, where he worked, where his dad and stepmother lived. But she wouldn't. If their roles had been reversed, she wouldn't have wanted to see him. He wouldn't have left if he thought they should be together.

No, she would wait to see if he changed his mind and came back to her. It needed to be his choice. She tried not to think about what she would do if he chose not to. She had no idea what her future would hold without him.

She closed her diary, closed her eyes, and hoped that he would forgive her.

*   *   *

What if he'd done the wrong thing? With the image of Ellie's sleeping face in his mind, Luke found it hard to believe that he had actually walked away. That he had got on a train and gone to Barcelona, to finally check into the hotel he had booked for his holiday. It was as terrible as the rest of the last minute deal had been, but it seemed to suit his mood.

Now that the morning had come and the effect of the vodka had worn off, he looked out at the view from his balcony (of a construction site across the road) and ran through the events of the previous two days. He could never in a million years have dreamed up what had happened. Had he really lived his life hundreds of times before? He didn't feel that way. As much as he felt an intense connection to Ellie, and a familiarity to her, if he hadn't read her diary, he would never have known where their relationship was going to go.

But he had read it. And now he knew that she really didn't want to be with him. She had tried hard to make it obvious when they'd met on the train, but he'd been oblivious. He didn't realise why she had tried to push him away. But he knew now. If they stayed together, she would die.

Luke recalled the list in her diary. The list of all her deaths. After the first twenty, he couldn't bring himself to read any more. In one life, they had even been killed at the same time. She believed that to break the cycle, to live longer than she had previously, and for him to live a long and happy life, she needed to avoid meeting him. That somehow, it would be a big enough change to alter the course of her destiny and his.

But despite everything, they had met. They had come together. So perhaps she was wrong? Luke's heart jumped for a moment. Maybe after the time they had spent together yesterday, she would see that she was wrong and change her mind.

Shaking his head, he went back inside and rummaged through the clothing he had packed in his suitcase, which had turned up at the hotel before he had. He picked out some clean clothing and headed for the shower. Thinking about it all was making his head spin. He needed to clear his mind for a bit. As he laid his clothes out ready and began to undress, he couldn't help but wonder if Ellie had found his note yet, and whether she was going to get in touch.

Though he couldn't bear the thought of her dying, he

was glad that he had left his number in her diary. Because if she changed her mind, if she thought that it could work, she could contact him.

He sighed and headed for the shower. All he could do now was wait.

*   *   *

"Hey, Mañana, you okay, sweetie?" Ellie whispered, as her cat rubbed up against her legs. It was several hours later and Ellie was still sat on the lounger, her diary on her lap, her body stiff from being so still.

She forced herself to get up and go to the kitchen. She searched through the cupboards and found the last tin of cat food. She fed Mañana, then after tucking her diary away in a drawer, she retrieved her handbag and headed for the door.

"I'll be back soon!" she called out to the cat as she left the house. Outside, she put her keys in her bag and set off, planning on getting the shopping done as quickly as possible, so that she could get home and hide for a while. She had no idea what to do now.

In all her lifetimes, she had never lived without Luke, and though she had been planning for years to avoid being with him, she'd never actually figured out what she would do if she was successful.

At the corner, she held out her hand to hail a taxi. When a car skidded to a stop beside her, she stepped inside.

"Supermercado, por favor."

"Not likely, sweetheart."

Ellie looked up just as the doors locked and a cloth covered her mouth.

*   *   *

Clean and showered, with a cocktail in hand, Luke sat next to the less than clean pool and tried to relax. He checked his phone for the hundredth time, and then wished he'd left it in his room. She wasn't going to call him. She would read his note, agree that it was better that they weren't together, and leave it at that. She was not going to call.

Movement to his left made him look up to see a bikini-clad girl walking toward him. He watched her settle on a lounger nearby, and it briefly crossed his mind that he should go and talk to her. After all, wasn't that the whole point of holidays? To meet random strangers and have some fun?

Of course, he had met Ellie. But from the moment he set eyes on her, he had known she wasn't a random stranger. She was something else entirely.

He'd never really believed in the concept of soulmates, but his encounter with Ellie had convinced him otherwise. He stopped watching the girl and turned his gaze back to the murky pool water. He checked his phone once more, then laid back and closed his eyes. Within seconds, he was asleep.

*   *   *

As soon as Ellie became aware of her body and her surroundings again, she fought the urge to start screaming and forced herself to breathe deeply and calmly, and assess the situation.

She was blind. There was a cloth of some sort tied so tightly around her head, that she couldn't even open her eyes. She also had tape across her mouth, and as she moved her hands fractionally, she deduced that she was also tied up. She was sitting upright, on something hard.

She breathed in and out of her nose, and listened hard to her surroundings. She couldn't hear any traffic, or any background noise of any sort. There was the occasional electrical hum, and muffled voices.

Still breathing calmly, Ellie wiggled a tiny bit more and found that her body was tied to what felt like a wooden chair, and her feet were also bound.

"Wakey wakey, rise and shine."

Ellie jumped at the rough voice that seemed to be coming from directly in front of her. She hadn't heard anyone else breathing, and didn't realise she was being watched.

There was a slow chuckle and Ellie's heart began to race as the situation finally sunk in.

"So then, darling, in a minute, I'm going to remove the tape and then you're going to start talking. I need to know names. The names of the people who are going to get you out of the sticky little mess that you're in right now. And contact numbers. Okay? Understand?"

Ellie didn't move, but a second later she gasped when the tape was ripped from her mouth, taking the skin from her lips at the same time.

"Speak," the voice said, lazily.

Ellie licked her lips, tasting the blood seeping from her raw flesh. She opened her mouth to speak, but nothing came out.

The blow to her ribs was so sudden that she didn't have time to catch her breath, and she sat gasping for air for a few seconds. When the voice spoke again, this time, the dangerous tone in his voice was plain.

"Speak."

Ellie managed to catch her breath and forced her words to come out. "There isn't anyone."

The blow this time was expected, but it still shocked

Ellie with its force and the pain that it caused her.

"I don't believe you. There must be someone who would pay for your release. There must be someone who cares whether you live or die."

Luke came to Ellie's mind, but she pushed him away. She couldn't think of Luke right now. He was gone. They weren't going to be together. It was better this way.

"There isn't anyone," Ellie repeated. "I have no family, and I've made a point of not making any friends."

There was a pause and Ellie waited for the next blow, but it didn't come.

"Why would you do that?" the voice asked. The menace seemed to have slipped slightly, and now Ellie could hear something like pity in it.

"Because I couldn't keep losing them. It's just too painful. Over and over I have had to lose the ones I have loved, and I vowed this time that I wouldn't do it. So I drove them all away."

"This time? I don't understand."

"That doesn't surprise me."

The slap across her cheek stung, but it hurt less than the earlier blows.

"Are you calling me stupid?" he demanded.

Ellie sighed. "No. I just wouldn't expect you to understand. No one has ever understood."

"Try me."

Ellie shrugged. Though she had no real desire to prolong the situation any longer than necessary, she wasn't in a great hurry to die, either. So she did her best to explain to her captor the concept that they were all living the same life over and over. Once she'd finished, there were a few minutes of silence, broken only by her own jagged breathing. It felt as though she may have a few broken ribs.

"What I don't understand is, if you've lived the same

life over and over, how did you let yourself be kidnapped?"

"Because it's never happened before. This time, in this life, some small things have changed."

"It all sounds a bit crazy to me. I think maybe you've been doing drugs or something."

Well, it wasn't a bad conclusion to come to, Ellie thought. She would assume the same thing if someone else had told her this story.

"What day is it today?" she asked.

"It's Wednesday."

Ellie struggled to remain patient. "And what's the date?"

"The sixth of July. Why?"

Ellie scanned the pages of her diary in her mind, looking for anything significant. An image jumped out at her of a double decker bus.

"What if I told you I could prove it? Would you let me go? I promise you that I have no family, no friends and no money. You could easily let me go, I haven't seen your face, so I couldn't identify you."

There was silence then, and Ellie held her breath.

"Okay, prove it, and I'll let you go."

Ellie let her breath out slowly, still hardly daring to hope. "Tomorrow morning, in London, there will be a terrorist attack. Three bombs will go off on the underground, and one bomb will blow up a double decker bus."

"How do you know that?"

"Because it happens every time."

"Okay, I guess we'll have to wait until tomorrow then." Tape was placed back over her mouth, and Ellie wished she had asked for a drink. As his footsteps left the room, she slumped in the chair. Now all she could do was wait. Though for what, she wasn't quite sure.

Chapter Six

Luke was drunk. It was a good thing that he had left Ellie, he decided, because she wouldn't have allowed him to drink so much. He was propped up at the end of the hotel bar, trying to explain to a fellow tourist what had happened to him on his holiday so far. But her glazed expression suggested that she didn't have a clue what Luke was talking about. He wasn't sure he knew either.

"She was gorgeous. Beautiful," he slurred. "More like a model than a real girl."

"And she was attracted to you?" the barman asked, his eyebrow raised.

Luke looked around and realised that his tourist friend had left, leaving him talking to himself. "I know. Unbelievable, right? So what did I do? I left. I thought she didn't want me, so I left."

"Women, they were invented purely to mess with your head."

Luke turned around and found himself squinting at the girl who had sat a few loungers away from him earlier in the day. "Exactly," he agreed. "That's right."

The girl laughed, then moved closer to him. "Would you like me to mess with your head a little more?"

Luke nodded, barely aware of his actions. He let the girl tug him from his bar stool and lead him out to the foyer. Somehow, she managed to get him into the lift and upstairs to her room. The last thing Luke remembered before slipping into a dark void was the sound of his jeans being unzipped.

*   *   *

Somehow, at some point, Ellie had fallen asleep, despite her very awkward position. She was rudely brought back to the present by another slap across the face.

"Hey, bitch. Wake up." Though just as menacing, it was a different voice to before. "My friend tells me that you're a psychic or something, and that you were trying to cut a deal for us to release you. I'm afraid I don't believe in all that bullshit, and I don't appreciate bitches trying to make deals with me. I'm in charge, I say what happens. So you either tell us the names of the people who will pay your ransom, or I'm going to kill you."

Ellie's heart thudded in her chest when Luke's face came into her mind again. She pushed it away and tried desperately to stay calm. She was prepared for it this time, but her lips stung as more flesh got ripped off.

"I already told your friend, there isn't anyone," she whispered. "And I'm not psychic. I just know what's going to happen because I've lived this life before. Many times."

"That's a real shame. I was hoping you would have a different answer for me."

Ellie heard the sound of a gun being cocked and her heart thudded to a halt. "Aren't you even going to wait until the morning to see if I was right?"

"Sorry, bitch. I've got better things to do."

Ellie swallowed hard and steeled herself for the moment she had experienced so many times before, though not quite in this way.

"I love you, Luke," she whispered, before the shot rang

out.

*   *   *

Luke jolted awake. He sat up and looked around him wildly.

"Ellie?"

"No, my name is Tiffany, what's yours?" came the sleepy reply.

Luke jumped out of the bed and got his legs tangled in the sheets, before landing on the floor in a heap. His head thudded painfully as he tried to untangle himself.

Tiffany peered over the edge of the bed and giggled at the sight of him. "What are you doing? It's way too early yet."

"What am I doing here?" Finally, Luke untangled himself and stood up, only then realising that he was naked. He looked at Tiffany and realised that she was also naked.

"Shit, did I, I mean, did we?" He shook his head then instantly regretted it. "It doesn't matter. I need to go." He grabbed his jeans and shirt from the floor and hastily put them on, nearly falling over again while Tiffany watched him in amusement.

"I'll see you later then?" she asked as he practically sprinted out of the door.

Heart hammering, Luke buttoned up his shirt as he strode barefoot down the hallway to the lift. He got in and went to his room, finding his key still in his jeans pocket along with his wallet. He let himself into his room and went straight to the phone on the bedside table.

Of course, there were no calls. He sat heavily on the edge of the bed, and after a few minutes, decided that he needed to leave Spain as soon as possible.

*   *   *

As Luke sat in the airport waiting for the next available flight, he watched the breaking news of the bombings in horror, temporarily forgetting his own problems. He glanced down at his phone for the millionth time. He wished she had just rung him to say goodbye. He didn't have any contact details for her. Part of him wished he had gone to her flat before coming to the airport, but he knew that he had to leave it up to her to contact him.

The security at the airport was understandably ridiculous when Luke arrived back in Heathrow, but he didn't even notice it. Rather than risk going into central London to get the train, he got on the next National Express from the airport. As the coach pulled away from the curb, he decided to just forget the whole holiday and forget that he had ever met Ellie. Or at least, he would try.

Part Two

Chapter Seven

"Ellie! Are you awake?"

Ellie opened her eyes and blinked rapidly. She was in her childhood bedroom, surrounded by stuffed animals and posters of her favourite books. She jumped out of bed and ran to the mirror, but she already knew what she would see.

The face of her six-year-old self stared back at her. She breathed heavily as the memory of her last life flashed through her mind. When she recalled waking up and finding Luke gone, she dropped to her knees on the pink carpet and cried.

"Ellie! What's wrong, sweetie?"

Ellie jumped up and threw herself into her mother's arms, seeking comfort from the woman who would soon be leaving her life yet again.

"What is it? Did you have a bad dream?" Ellie nodded into her mother's soft shoulder. "Do you want to tell me about it?"

Ellie shook her head.

"You could try writing it down, would you like that?"

Ellie nodded again, and her mother left the room, returning a few moments later with a very familiar small brown leather diary.

"Try writing them in here. It might help." She kissed Ellie on the forehead, and left her to start writing down all of the memories from her many lives.

*   *   *

The years passed by, yet Ellie still hadn't formed any kind of plan. Should she try to avoid meeting Luke this time, or should she let things happen like they normally did, but just not tell him everything?

Her days were consumed with thoughts of her impending future. Soon, at least, she would be able to leave school and set out on her own. She had breezed through her classes and used all of the spare time she had to write more notes in her diary, the one her mother had given her ten years before. She sighed and stared out of the classroom window. It still hurt to think about her mother. No matter how many times she went through the experience of losing her, it was still painful. Living with her aunt was okay, but they weren't very close.

Somehow, she got through another mindless day and was walking home from school when she saw the lady from across the street waving at her. She had always avoided conversations with her, as she had been said to have psychic abilities. Ellie already knew more than enough about the future and she didn't need anyone else to remind her of what was to come.

But today, Ellie changed her mind. She crossed the street and greeted her neighbour.

"Hello, Mrs Mackey. Have you had a good day?"

"Ellie. I'm so glad you finally changed your mind."

Ellie was taken aback by her neighbour's tone of voice. "What do you mean?"

"Come inside and have a cup of tea with me."

Ellie bit her lip. "I should get home, I have homework."

"Which I'm sure will take you all of about five minutes.

I won't take up too much of your time, but I know that you will be glad you came in."

Ellie shrugged and nodded. She followed Mrs Mackey into her house, surprised to find that it was airy and modern, not at all like a psychic's house. Though what a psychic's house should look like, Ellie wasn't quite sure.

Mrs Mackey gestured to a chair by the kitchen table, then got them both a cup of tea and some biscuits. Ellie sat down and started nibbling on the edge of a biscuit, suddenly famished.

She became aware of Mrs Mackey watching her, and despite her hunger, she put the half-eaten biscuit back on her plate.

"I wish you had come to me sooner, my dear Ellie. I could have saved you so much pain."

Ellie shook her head. "I don't understand what you mean."

"This must be at least your hundredth time, living this life?"

Ellie's eyes widened and she stared at Mrs Mackey. "How do you know that?"

Mrs Mackey smiled. "I know many things."

"But no one ever believed me, so I stopped saying anything. I haven't told a soul in this lifetime."

"I know. But you have come to me now, that's the important thing."

"You said you could help me. How?"

"I cannot tell you how to live, Ellie, but I can tell you this: you would do best if you lived in the present. I know it is difficult for you to let go of the past and, my dear, you have had far more of a past than anyone else. But you have to let it go. Similarly, you have to let go of the future. You cannot change the future with your thoughts fixed firmly on the past. Do you understand?"

Ellie frowned. "I think so. Do you remember all of your lives too?"

"My dear Ellie. Your beliefs about the way reincarnation works aren't quite right. The reason you are the only one who remembers living your life over and over, is because you are the only one doing so."

"So it doesn't work that way for everyone? I'm the only one living their life over and over? But how can that be? Why am I doomed to live the same life again and again?"

Mrs Mackey sighed. "I'm afraid we have so much work to do and your choice of words is not helping you at all."

"My choice of words?"

"Yes. You are not 'doomed' to live your life over and over. You chose to do so."

"I chose to? When? I don't remember choosing this nightmare."

"Ellie, please think about the words you are using. Every word you speak or think is creating your future. You must be so careful with what you are saying."

"Creating my future? How can I create my future? It's already set! There's nothing I can do to change it." Ellie stood up. She didn't care now that Mrs Mackey believed her, she was leaving.

"You changed things last time."

Ellie paused and frowned. "But not for the better. My life just ended a few years sooner than normal."

"But it means that change is possible."

Ellie sat back down again. "Are you saying that I really can change the ending? I can change my fate?"

Mrs Mackey smiled. "I am saying that you need to let go of the past and the future and focus on the present. That you need to be aware of every word you speak, write and say, because those words are creating your life. If you wish to learn with me, I would love to help you, Ellie."

Ellie sat quietly for a few minutes, then picked up the biscuit again.

"I'm listening."

*   *   *

"So this is it?"

Ellie nodded and reluctantly handed over her diary to Mrs Mackey, who she had started calling Mrs M.

Mrs M took the diary and placed it on the table between them. "Are you sure you haven't stored any memories anywhere else?"

"Other than in my own mind, no, I haven't. They're all in there." Ellie looked at the brown leather diary, full of the words and drawings that encapsulated the events of all the lives that she could remember. Just that morning she had re-read the part where she had met Luke and told him everything. She wondered what had happened to him after she had died. Did he even know about her death? Did he even care? Ellie shook her head and made herself focus on the present moment again.

Mrs M smiled. "Welcome back. Where were you that time?"

Ellie blushed. "I was just thinking of the last time I saw Luke."

Mrs M shook her head. "That's why we need to do this. Once you have cleansed your life of these memories, you can begin to move on in earnest."

Ellie sighed. "I'm not sure about this," she whispered. "What if I'm supposed to remember, what if there's a reason for it?"

"If you haven't figured out the reason after all these lives, I think it might be safe to assume otherwise. If you're not ready to begin creating the life you wish for, then perhaps we should postpone this."

"No, I'm ready. I need to do this. I can't live this life yet again. I need to change it. For the better."

"Okay then. Let's go outside."

Out in the back garden, there was an old metal dustbin, with papers and twigs inside. Mrs M handed the diary back to Ellie, then lit the rubbish. After a few minutes, there was a healthy blaze throwing heat toward them.

Ellie looked down at her diary. Then taking in a deep breath, she opened the diary to the first page, and ripped it out. She screwed it up into a ball and threw it into the bin. She watched it flare up and burn for a few seconds, then something seemed to take over her, and suddenly she was ripping several pages out at once and throwing them into the flames. Beside her, Mrs M was murmuring words of encouragement.

After a few frenzied moments, Ellie found herself holding just the final page and the cover in her hands. Just as she threw them into the fire, she thought she saw words and a phone number appear on the page, but the fire consumed them before she could make sure.

Ellie wasn't aware of the tears running down her face until she felt Mrs M's arm around her and she dissolved into sobs.

*   *   *

"What you did today was the first step toward creating a new life for yourself. By getting rid of your past and future memories, you have cleared the way to create new ones."

Ellie fiddled with the edge of the tablecloth and stared at the geometric pattern. It didn't feel like she'd taken the first step toward anything, it felt more like she had lost everything, again.

"Ellie, I know you are grieving the loss of all you have experienced before, but it's necessary to release the past before you can move on and create a new life." Mrs M reached across the table and patted Ellie's hand. "You have more memories than most to release, so it may seem harder for you to do so. But once you do, I promise that you will feel lighter. And free."

Ellie nodded, still not trusting herself to speak. Even after working with Mrs M for this last week, she still found it hard not to dwell on the past, and the possible futures. How was she supposed to forget it all?

"By staying present at all times."

Ellie looked up. She didn't know if she had spoken aloud or if Mrs M had read her mind. She decided it didn't matter and sat up straight.

"I'm here."

"Here is all there is."

*   *   *

The world was such a different place when you remained in the present moment. Ellie walked down the street to Mrs M's house, and was struck by the incredible beauty that surrounded her. The sky was a clear deep blue, the lawns she passed were a bright, lush green. She felt like she had never experienced and appreciated colour like this before. Not that she recalled what things were like before. No, right now she was in the very present moment, feeling the pavement under the thin soles of her shoes, feeling the breeze in her hair, and feeling the warmth of the sun on her face.

She reached Mrs M's house and let herself in. After two years of working with her, Ellie had become more like family than a client or even a friend.

"Hey, Mrs M, I'm here," she called out as she hung her light jacket and her bag in the hallway. She took out her new diary, the one that she had been filling with words and sketches and even the odd photograph of what she wanted her life to be like. They had been working on it more often recently. Mrs M was always telling her that the clearer she was about the things that she wanted to experience, the more likely she was to actually experience them.

She stepped into the lounge and blinked in surprise. In all the time she had known Mrs M, she had never known the tiny television to be switched on. And she had certainly never expected to ever see Mrs M watching it so intently.

"Mrs M?" No response. She walked over to her friend and gently laid a hand on her shoulder. Before she could speak again, her gaze was finally drawn to the images on the tiny, flickering screen.

Her stomach lurched and she swallowed hard. How could she have forgotten this? Suddenly all of her present moment awareness disappeared and she remembered reliving the events of this particular day over and over in her many lifetimes. In one lifetime, she had even tried to report the events to the police in the USA, but they hadn't taken her seriously. She'd spent a year in a tiny place in Switzerland after that, living under a different name. She was worried that they might think she'd had something to do with the terrorist attacks.

She squeezed Mrs M's shoulder gently, and finally the older woman looked up at her.

"I knew something was going to happen today. I've been having visions for weeks. But I never knew it would be this bad."

Ellie sighed. "I can't believe I actually forgot it was going to happen. For so many lifetimes, the numbers of today's date were imprinted on my mind." She gave Mrs

M a half-smile. "It shows how good your present moment training is though, doesn't it?"

Mrs M tried to smile back. "I suppose you're right." With a sigh she got up and switched the TV off. "I shall just have to send out positive thoughts to those affected. And pray for those who have caused it."

Ellie nodded. She hated that there was no more they could do than that, but she knew, better than anyone, that there were some things you just couldn't change. "I tried to change it once," she said quietly. "It didn't make any difference." She tilted her head and looked Mrs M straight in the eye. "So what makes you so sure that I can change things this time?"

Mrs M kept the eye contact. "Because you are ready to."

*   *   *

Later that evening, Ellie was sat on her bed in her tiny room, looking through the diary of her ideal life. She had written statements of how she felt, what she did, who she was. She had written diary entries about her life, in the present tense. She had drawn little sketches of what her house looked like, what her bedroom looked like, and even the view she had from her bedroom window. Every night, before going to sleep, she read her diary from cover to cover, looking at the pictures, absorbing every detail, sometimes adding new detail as she learned more about the kind of life she wanted to experience.

Her memories of previous lives were slowly fading, slowly being rewritten by the desires held within her diary. And each day felt new, it felt like she was being spontaneous and following her intuition, rather than just copying her past actions. She had even started dressing differently and had grown her hair out, it now reached her waist in soft waves.

She felt like she was becoming the person she was always meant to be. She was becoming a person who valued every moment, and who was present in every moment.

Mrs M had a great method for becoming present when she found herself getting lost in her memories. All she had to do was ask herself three questions and she would become present once more.

"Am I alive? Am I awake? Am I loved?" These would then be transformed into three positive statements - "I am alive. I am awake. I am loved."

Ellie had lost count of the number of times she had repeated those questions and statements to herself. They were quite effective and she found that her worries and memories would slip away instantly, leaving her to concentrate on whatever the present moment held. It amazed her how often people missed out on the good stuff because they were so wrapped up in the bad stuff that had happened long before, or that had yet to happen.

Her mind briefly wandered to the events of the day. No matter how many times she had experienced it, it still upset her deeply. The lives that had been lost, the devastation that had been caused. But it seemed that the larger events were out of her hands. If indeed she was the only one living her life over and over, as Mrs M seemed to think, then the only life she could really affect was her own. And perhaps the lives of those closest to her.

She finished reading her diary, and turned to a clean page. She had been putting off writing about her ideal relationship until now, because her memories of Luke had still been so clear. But it was time. Time to create the kind of relationship that she wanted to experience in her new life. If that relationship was going to be with someone other than Luke, then perhaps that would be a good thing.

My ideal partner is... Ellie stared at the words, her pen hovering above the page. She closed her eyes, and breathed in deeply. Once her mind was clear and she was in the present moment, she opened her eyes and began to write.

Chapter Eight

"May I sit here?"

Ellie didn't even look up from her novel. She moved her bag from the seat beside her and continued reading. She had reached a critical point in the story and refused to be derailed from it.

But his scent was unmistakeable. She breathed it in and found herself transported to a hundred other moments that had started in this way, with this man. She blinked rapidly, unable to focus on the words of her novel. She waited for him to speak, but the minutes and the scenery rolled by and he didn't utter a word. She peered sideways at him and saw that he was engrossed in a book by one of Mrs M's favourite authors. Ellie had also read the book, she had read all of the author's books in fact, and thought they were incredible. She glanced up quickly at his face and frowned.

He looked different. Though it was definitely Luke, his face had changed. She had never seen him look so healthy before. So relaxed. Suddenly he looked at her and caught her staring at him. He started to look away, but then frowned and looked back at her.

"Hey," he said. "Have we met before?"

Ellie smiled, and remembering her promise to stay in the present moment, at all times, she shook her head. "No, I don't think we have."

He tilted his head. "Okay, well, hi, my name's Luke."

Ellie held her hand out to him. "Ellie. Nice to meet you, Luke."

Luke took her hand and shook it. Ellie nearly laughed at the formality of their encounter, compared to the familiarity of his touch. He released her hand and closed his book. "So where are you going, Ellie?"

"To London. There's a Mind, Body, Spirit Festival on at-"

"Olympia. How funny, that's where I'm heading, too."

Ellie's eyes widened. "Seriously?"

Luke laughed. "Yeah, why does that seem strange?"

Ellie shook her head. "I don't know, I just didn't think you seemed like the type to go to that sort of thing."

Luke held up his book. "What, even though I'm reading this? What type of person did you think I was?"

"I don't know, the type who would have a normal job, not much interest in the mystical or paranormal, who drinks too much, is really neat and nit-picky and who wants to travel around the world." Ellie blurted it all out before she could stop to think through what she was saying.

Luke's eyebrows raised. "You got all that from sitting next to me for less than five minutes? Wow, I must put more effort into the energy I'm sending out. I'm afraid to say I don't think you're psychic. I'm very much in tune with the mystical, I work as a healer in a Spiritual Centre, and I don't drink alcohol, take drugs or smoke. I don't mind a little mess and I have already travelled the world, so I guess I have to give you that one, sort of."

Ellie was speechless. This was not the Luke she knew. This was not the same man she had spent countless lives with, this was the man she had dreamed of being with, when she created her ideal relationship in her diary, four years earlier.

"I do apologise, Luke. I shouldn't have made such assumptions about you, I had no right."

Luke chuckled. "No need to be so serious, Ellie. It's fine. I'm just curious as to why you made those assumptions. Is it the way I'm dressed? The way I talk?"

Ellie took in his appearance properly, and saw that he wasn't even dressed the way he would have been in the past. Instead of the uniform of jeans and a t-shirt, he had a loose Renaissance-style shirt on, with baggy linen trousers. She shook her head. "No, I guess it must have been because you reminded me of someone I knew a long time ago."

"Oh, that's good. I wouldn't want people to think I was an anally retentive alcoholic or something."

Ellie blushed and looked down at her forgotten novel.

Luke reached across and patted her hand, sending Ellie's nervous system into overdrive. She glanced up to see the expression on his face.

"Do you do energy work?" he asked. "Because I swear I just got an electric shock from you."

Ellie smiled then looked up at him. "I've done a little. Mainly I just practice being in the present moment, by noticing all that is happening here and now, and not getting lost in my memories or in my worries."

Luke nodded. "That sounds like a great thing to practice. I've been meditating for years now, but I'm not sure I'll ever get to the point of living purely in the present."

Ellie raised an eyebrow. "If you talk in that way, I wouldn't be surprised if you never did."

"You're right. I just mentioned the past and the future and negated the present all in one sentence, didn't I?"

"Yep, you did."

"Sorry. I'll try not to do it again."

"Future."

"What?"

"It's what Mrs M would say to me. Any time I used the future tense, she'd just say 'future' and if I mentioned the past, she'd say 'past'. It was quite effective. Certainly made a lot of our conversations very short, too."

"Mrs M? Was she your mentor?"

"Yes, and my friend too." Ellie sighed. "She passed away last year."

"Oh, I'm sorry. You must miss her?"

"Every day. But her lessons have stayed with me. As hard as it was to not get lost in the grief of losing yet another person I loved, I stayed present, and every day I thank the universe for bringing us together."

"She did a good job with you, I think. I've never met anyone who is so grounded and so positive."

"Thank you. She was an excellent teacher."

"So are you worried about being in London?"

"Worried? You mean because of last week's events? I must admit, I nearly didn't come," Ellie admitted. "But then I realised I was being silly. I'll just stay away from the tube and double deckers."

Luke frowned. "Yeah, I can't quite believe what happened. Seems a little unreal."

"I know what you mean." Ellie looked out the window and realised that the train had come to a stop a few moments before.

"Wow, that was quick." She tucked her novel into her handbag and stood up.

"I don't know if you want company, but in light of recent events, could I escort you to the Festival?"

Ellie smiled at his formal courteousness. "I would love that."

They gathered their suitcases and left the carriage.

"So tell me something about yourself, Ellie."

"What would you like to know?"

"Surprise me."

*   *   *

Luke looked into her eyes as she laughed and couldn't believe his luck. Their connection had been instant and undeniable, and he felt like he had finally found the missing ingredient to a happy life.

He had only spent five hours and thirty-three minutes with Ellie (okay so he was actually a little anal about some things, but he wasn't going to admit that now) and already he couldn't imagine his life without her. She was funny and spontaneous, yet intense at the same time. She was also absolutely gorgeous. He loved her long, wavy hair, her brightly coloured clothes and her cheeky smile.

"So what do you think?"

Luke blinked. He had been so lost in his thoughts that he had not heard her previous sentence. He held his hands up. "I'm sorry, I was lost in my thoughts and not here with you. What do I think about what?"

Ellie smiled. "Don't worry, I'll let you off just this once. I was asking if you fancied having dinner later, after the Festival? I'm staying with a friend in Putney, but she's not expecting me until much later anyway."

Luke nodded. "That sounds good. I've got a hotel room booked just down the road. Perhaps we could dump our stuff there, get a bite to eat, then I can take you to your friend's house?"

"That sounds like a plan. Now, enough future stuff." Ellie stood up and picked up her empty cup and cake wrapper. "I need to find the perfect pendulum."

Luke followed her lead, taking his own rubbish to the

nearest bin.

"Let's do it."

*   *   *

"So where did it begin for you, your spiritual journey?" Ellie asked, as she placed her napkin on her lap. Luke settled in his chair opposite her and did the same.

"I've never told anyone how it started, because it's a bit crazy."

"I'm sure it's not that bad."

Luke shrugged. "Okay, don't say I didn't warn you. I was in my office cubicle, just mindlessly doing what I did every day since I'd left school – inputting data, analysing data, blah blah, and suddenly out of nowhere, a thought struck me."

Ellie nodded for him to continue. "What was it?"

"I suddenly thought, what if this isn't the first time I've lived this life, what if it's the hundredth?"

Ellie nearly choked on the sip of water she'd just taken. "What?" she whispered.

"I know, it's a weird concept, but it suddenly made me realise that if this was in fact my hundredth time of living my life, then I sure as hell didn't want it to be the same as all the others. It gave me a sense of freedom to really think about what I wanted. And I literally stopped typing, stood up, got my coat, walked out of the office and never returned."

Ellie's eyebrows shot up. "What did you do then?"

"I went home, booked a round the world ticket, packed my bags and left the next day."

"Wow. That is really quite incredible."

Luke smiled. "I guess it seems so now, but to me, it would have been impossible to do anything else. I just couldn't have stayed in that job. I was wasting my life by being stressed out over things that essentially didn't matter."

"Still, I'm impressed. What did your family say?" Ellie recalled a vague memory of Luke's dad and stepmother, and they weren't the type of people to endorse such spontaneous behaviour.

"They were mad, at first. But when I came back from my trip six months later, I think they realised how much it had changed my life, and they accepted it then. In fact, it even inspired them to go travelling more themselves."

"Can I take your order?"

Ellie jumped a little and looked up at the waiter. She hadn't even noticed him standing there.

"I'll have the spinach and feta lasagne, please."

Luke nodded. "I'll have the same, and could we have a side order of salad as well?"

The waiter nodded and left, taking their menus with him.

"Do you know the most amazing thing I learned, while on my travels?"

Ellie shook her head.

"Before my wake-up call, I'd always assumed that stress was just a normal part of life. An essential part, even. But when I left everything behind and travelled around the world, I realised that stress was actually only possible when you held the belief of lack."

"The belief of lack?"

"Yes, when you believe that there's a lack of anything - time, money, love, etcetera - that's when you suffer from stress. It's actually impossible to experience stress when you know and believe that the universe is a friendly and abundant place. When you know that everything happens at the perfect time, in the perfect way."

Their food arrived and they both started eating. The lasagne tasted better than anything Ellie had ever eaten before. She wondered if it was because she was so present in the moment, or if it was because of the company she was in.

It wasn't long before they had dessert in front of them and they were both enjoying and savouring every bite, appreciating the flavours and textures of the food.

"So how did your journey begin?" Luke asked, as he wiped his mouth with his napkin.

"My journey? I live in Worcester."

Luke chuckled. "I meant your spiritual journey."

Ellie swallowed her mouthful of chocolate fudge cake and giggled. "Of course you did, I'm sorry. Um, I guess it started when I met Mrs M."

"Tell me more about her, she sounds interesting. How did she become your tutor?"

Ellie shrugged. "By chance, really. She was psychic, and she said she could help me. So I started going over to her house every day, and she taught me present moment awareness."

"She woke you up?"

"In a way, yes. She helped me to stay present. I had spent my whole life up to that point in the past and the future. Writing about it, thinking about it, dreading what was going to happen."

"The future? Are you really psychic then?"

Ellie started to shake her head, then decided to have a little fun. "A little bit, yeah."

"Are you clairvoyant? Clairsentient?"

"A bit of everything really. I see visions of events, I feel things and have even been known to hear voices." Ellie knew she should stop, but for once it was nice to make light of her situation.

"That's really cool. Are you sensing anything about me?"

Ellie tilted her head to one side, squinted a little, pretending to read him while she dug into her memories for some suitable information to impart.

"I can see a small dog. He's black and white, and I'm hearing the name 'Sam'. Perhaps he was your dog when you were a child?"

At the sight of Luke's wide eyes and gaping mouth, Ellie nearly lost her act and started giggling. He nodded and she tilted her head to the other side.

"I can see a house by the sea. It's white, quite small, with roses around the doorway. I get the feeling that a relative of yours lived there, and you used to visit them every summer."

Luke's mouth opened and closed several times, but no sound came out. Ellie stopped squinting at him and smiled. "Was I right?" she asked innocently.

Luke nodded, still in a state of shock. Finally he found his voice again. "I've been to see psychics, and they've given me a lot of information, most of it about the future, most of which didn't happen. But none of them has come out with such accurate information about my past before. There are very few people on the planet who even know about Sam, I only had him for a year before he was hit by a car and killed."

Ellie winced. She'd forgotten that bit. She wouldn't have mentioned him if she had remembered. She reached over and put her hand over his. "I'm sorry, Luke. But I'm sure that he's happy on the other side. I'm sure he remembers how well you looked after him."

Luke smiled. "Thank you, Ellie. I really did love him. But you're right, I'm sure he's doing well wherever he is."

Ellie took her hand back and finished her dessert. Luke

motioned for the waiter to bring them the bill.

"Would you like to come back to my hotel room for a drink?"

Ellie nodded. "I have to come back with you to get my luggage anyway, but I would like a drink, yes. I'll just ring my friend on the way to let her know I'll be there later."

Luke paid the bill and they left the restaurant. It was only a short walk to the hotel, but a chilly breeze had picked up, making Ellie shiver. Luke put his arm around her and held her close as they walked.

Ellie smiled. Though he had changed in so many ways, she knew then that his feelings for her had most definitely stayed the same.

*   *   *

"So, are you going to give me your phone number?" Luke asked, as they waited in Paddington station for Ellie's train.

Ellie looked up at him. "I would have been able to find you, you know. I *am* psychic." She tapped the side of her head and raised an eyebrow.

"I'm sure you would, but just in case, let's swap phone numbers."

Ellie sighed. "Are you saying you don't trust my awesome powers?" She shook her head and made an elaborate show of tapping her phone number into his phone. She handed the phone back to him and a second later, her own phone started vibrating in her pocket.

"Now you have my number, too."

"And now you know I didn't give you a fake number," Ellie added, a grin on her face.

Luke laughed. "Yeah, that has happened to me a few times, actually."

The train arrived and Ellie's stomach lurched. After

spending the weekend with the new and improved Luke, she couldn't imagine being without him now.

She saw in his eyes that he was thinking the same.

"Can we meet up soon?" he asked.

Ellie nodded, then moved closer to him. Finally, after she had waited all weekend, he leaned in and kissed her. All rational thought left her mind, and nothing other than this moment existed. Ellie now truly understood the concept of present moment awareness.

Too quickly, the moment passed and his lips left hers. She kept her eyes closed a moment longer, hoping to prolong it.

"I'll call you soon, Ellie. I'm so very glad we met."

She nodded and tried not to show him how much it hurt to walk away. She reached the door of the train, and looked back, but he was already gone.

$$* \qquad * \qquad *$$

His vision blurred as he walked out of the train station and back to the hotel.

The sights and sounds that surrounded him held no meaning; all he could think of was how much he missed her already. He had never before felt such a deep connection to another human being. When their lips had met just seconds before she walked away, he felt like he had simultaneously come home and had discovered what had been missing from his life.

She was the one.

He was as certain of that as he was of his own name.

When he finally brought himself out of his thoughts and into the present moment, he realised that he was stood in front of his hotel. As he climbed the steps he wished he could have travelled back with her, but he had been planning the next week for several months. He had managed to pack in as many spiritual talks and workshops into one week as was possible, and he was looking forward to learning from all of the spiritual masters and authors.

He entered the lift and stared blindly at his reflection in the lift doors. He didn't recognise himself. He had changed so much in the last three days.

When he reached his hotel room, he swiped the key card and entered. He collapsed onto the neatly made bed and wondered what Ellie was thinking right that second.

Without thinking it through, he pulled his phone out and called the last number dialled on his list.

"Hello?" Her quiet voice was nearly drowned out by the noise of the train.

"I couldn't wait any longer, I had to hear your voice." He thought he heard her sigh, and wondered if that was a good thing.

"I'm so glad you called. I miss you already, too."

Luke smiled. "What are you doing next Saturday?"

*   *   *

"Do you think we're moving too fast?"

Ellie looked up at Luke as he made breakfast in his tiny kitchen. She looked down at her attire - she was wearing nothing but one of his soft Renaissance-style shirts - then she looked back at him again and smiled. "Why would you think that?"

Luke laughed. "We met, what, eight days ago, and here you are, in my flat, naked, having just spent the night." He shrugged. "By my standards, that's pretty fast."

"I'm not naked. Are you trying to imply that I'm easy?" Ellie teased.

Luke set the knife down and went over to her. He

wrapped his arms around her waist and squeezed gently. "Of course not, I just don't want to take things too quickly and end up scaring you away."

"You couldn't scare me if you tried, Luke. Trust me."

"I do trust you." Luke kissed her on top of her head and released her, returning to his breakfast preparations.

She walked into his living area and flopped onto the sofa. She shifted to one side and pulled out the remote control she'd sat on. She pressed the button and switched on the TV. Part of her was surprised that the new Luke actually owned a TV, but she knew that the old Luke wouldn't be able to survive without his weekly fix of sports.

The screen flickered on, revealing a newswoman behind a desk. The first words she spoke made Ellie's heart stop.

"Just this morning, the body of an unidentified young woman was found a few miles outside of the Spanish city of Lerida. It appears that she was shot in the head."

The newswoman continued, and Ellie sat frozen on the sofa. Her hands started to shake and she dropped the remote. Her mind flashed back to her buried memories of the two men who had tied her up and held her captive, before killing her.

Had she really changed her fate? Or had her fate simply been passed on to some other poor, unsuspecting victim?

Ellie didn't even hear Luke enter the room or set the breakfast tray on the coffee table. She jumped when his hand touched her shoulder.

"Ellie, what's wrong? Why are you crying?"

Ellie touched her face and realised it was wet. She hadn't been aware of her own tears.

The newswoman had moved on to the next item. Luke picked up the remote and switched the TV off. He gently gripped her shoulders and turned her to face him.

"Ellie, what is it?"

*   *   *

As Luke waited for her to answer, his mind was racing through hundreds of possibilities. Was she regretting last night? Did she wish they hadn't met? He resisted the urge to ask her again, and breathed deeply to calm his fears.

Finally, she looked up at him, and seemed to focus. "It's silly, really. There was something on the news that upset me."

Luke frowned. She looked like she was in a deep state of shock, not just a little upset. "Really? What was it?"

Ellie shook her head. "It doesn't matter."

"Was it about what happened in London the other week?"

She shook her head again. "No, it doesn't matter. It just surprised me, that's all. I'm fine now." She gave him an unconvincing smile and reached out to take her plate from the tray. Luke noticed her hands were shaking, but didn't say anything. He knew that she wasn't telling him the whole story, but he trusted her, and knew she would tell him if it was something he needed to know.

They ate breakfast in silence, and slowly Luke noticed Ellie's colour returning and her hands become still. Whatever she had seen on the TV had seriously shaken her. Luke couldn't help but feel a little relieved that her tears hadn't had anything to do with him, though.

They spent the rest of the day talking. Luke learned more about Mrs M and how she had helped Ellie.

Ellie asked him about his spiritual journey, and he described the people he had met, and the realisations he'd had while travelling the world.

He also told her about the talks he'd attended in

London. By the end of the week all of the information had blurred together; but he said he felt a lot lighter, and a lot more in control of his destiny.

"What do you mean, you feel in control of your destiny?" Ellie asked.

"I mean, I feel like I'm choosing my life, and not just accepting whatever comes my way."

"So you think that you chose to meet me? That it wasn't fate or destiny choosing for you?"

"Yes, I think I chose to meet you. And I don't know about you, but I felt a connection instantly."

Ellie bit her lip, and Luke wondered again what she was thinking.

"What if you didn't choose to meet me? What if you were destined to meet me, and there was nothing you could do to stop it?"

Luke considered it for a few seconds, then smiled. "It doesn't matter. Because I'm glad that I met you. Whether it was fate or not, I wouldn't change it."

*   *   *

Her earlier shock had worn off, and after several hours of talking, Ellie rested comfortably in Luke's arms on the sofa. She sent out prayers for the girl who had been murdered in Spain. And to the girl's family. She felt awful that it had happened, but she couldn't help but feel relieved that it wasn't her this time.

Luke had suggested going out for dinner, but Ellie just wanted to stay in and get to know him better. He had changed so much. Though she tried to follow Mrs M's advice and stay in the present moment, her mind was whirling with all of the past and future possibilities. She wondered what had happened to Luke in their previous time together, after she had been killed. Had he found out about her death? Had he lived to be an old man? Had losing her caused his complete change of character in this life?

She had still never managed to get her head around the fact that it was only she who was experiencing her life over and over. Because if that was the case, then Luke wouldn't have had any recollection of their previous time together, so surely he would have remained the same as ever? How was it that he had changed this time?

Luckily, Luke had lapsed into silence too, otherwise she would never have been able to keep up a conversation.

Her mind continued to whirl with all of the possibilities and she wished that she had someone she could speak to about it. But she couldn't tell Luke. Not this time. The last time had not ended well at all. At least she knew that it couldn't happen that way again, because she no longer had the diary that had pushed him away. Her diary was now filled with positive affirmations and positive experiences. She hadn't written anything negative in it at all. Even when she had been upset, she had turned her thoughts of despair into prayers. Her desire in this life, was to be happy and positive, with a happy, positive and spiritual partner by her side.

She looked up at Luke and realised that he'd fallen asleep. She couldn't bear the thought of leaving him tomorrow. Of going home to her own little flat. Her heart ached at the thought of being away from him.

"Luke," she whispered. He stirred a little then, his eyelids flickered at the sound of his name. "Luke, I don't want to go home. I want to stay here, with you."

The smile on his face told her all she needed to know. He squeezed her gently. "Then stay."

"Okay."

Chapter Nine

Luke was trying to meditate, but his mind was running wild. He kept thinking about the previous six months, which had been the best of his life. Ellie had moved into his flat, and had put hers up for sale. Soon they were in perfect sync with each other. Due to several inheritances, then the sale of her flat, Ellie didn't actually need to work, but she started doing a few hours at the meditation centre where Luke worked. She was a natural meditator, and had helped other people who were having difficulties with it.

The other reason he figured he was having difficulty clearing his mind, was because he knew she was in the building right now. He could sense her presence even though she was several rooms away. They were so in tune with each other, they always knew what the other was going to say or do. But one thing had remained unsolved, and Luke could feel it as an actual entity between them. There was something that Ellie wasn't telling him. Something major.

Luke sighed and shifted slightly, but quietly, so as not to interrupt his student's meditation. He wished Ellie would confide in him. Whatever the knowledge was, it seemed to weigh her down. He knew it would lighten her burden if she shared it with him. He had tried to approach the subject many times, but she had refused to open up to him. Once, he felt like she had been close to telling him, that the words were right there, just waiting to burst out, but she'd reined them in at the last second.

Luke breathed deeply. Thinking about it wasn't going to help him right now. He needed to focus, and be in the present.

He took another deep breath, and tried to let go.

*   *   *

Ellie was whistling a quiet, happy tune to herself as she cleaned the meditation room ready for her next class. The space was already spotless, but Ellie always liked to clean the room energetically between sessions, to make sure that nothing lingered after her students had released their fears and worries.

She brushed the floor rhythmically, imagining all of the negative energies dissipating harmlessly, when suddenly she felt a presence behind her. She whirled around and came face to face with a man.

His eyes widened as he looked at her. She frowned. She didn't recognise him, from this life or any other, but he was so familiar to her, she felt as though she should.

"You know, don't you?" he whispered, taking a step forward. "I can sense it. I can see it in your eyes. You know."

"I know what?" Ellie asked, though she knew what his answer was going to be.

"That this is not the only time we have lived this life. That we live it over and over."

Ellie dropped the broom and it clattered to the wooden floor. "You're an Elphite too?"

"A what?"

Ellie blushed. She'd never told anyone the name she'd called herself before. "An Elphite. Someone who remembers living their life over and over."

"I didn't know it had a name, but yes, I do remember. I have lived my life so many times. It never ends. I've tried, but I can't make it end."

The desperation in his voice made Ellie's heart clench. She knew the feeling well. But she had long since transmuted it into a feeling of wonder, rather than pain.

"Though it doesn't seem to have affected you as much? Have you not lived it many times yet?" The man was closing the gap now, his piercing gaze staring at her, taking in her whole appearance.

Ellie shook her head. "I've lived it many times, but this time I changed things."

"Changed things? What do you mean? You cannot change things, it remains the same, every time." The man stopped then, and blinked. "Though, this has never happened before. We have never met before. This *is* different. How have you done this?"

Movement behind the man caught Ellie's eye and she looked over his shoulder to see the rest of her students enter the room. "We can continue this conversation after class. I think there's a lot we can learn from each other."

The man nodded, and went to take his place on a mat near the front. Ellie picked up the broom and set it against the wall. She greeted her students and took her place at the front of the room. She took a deep breath, and tried to empty her mind of the previous few minutes. Then she began the class.

*   *   *

"Luke?"

Luke looked up and couldn't stop the grin that spread across his face. He strode across the room and wrapped his arms around Ellie, kissing her passionately. For once though, Ellie didn't return the kiss. She pulled back a little and Luke then saw the man stood behind her.

"Sorry, can I help you?" he asked.

"Luke, this is Elijah. He was in my class this morning."

Luke reached out and shook Elijah's hand.

"Hello, Elijah, I hope you enjoyed the class. Is it your first time here?"

Elijah nodded, but didn't quite meet his gaze. Luke tried to keep his face expressionless, but was confused. "Are we still good for tonight?" he asked Ellie.

"Actually, that's why we popped by. Elijah and I have a few things to discuss, so we were thinking of going out for a meal."

Luke couldn't stop his eyebrows from raising. "Oh, I see. Okay. I'll see you later then?"

Ellie nodded, but she too couldn't quite meet his eye.

Luke was not a jealous person, nor was he suspicious or untrusting, but he knew that there was a lot more to this exchange than Ellie was letting on. He leaned forward to kiss Ellie on the cheek and she smiled at him.

"I'll see you at home."

Luke nodded and she walked away, Elijah just a step behind her. He trusted her implicitly, but he wasn't so sure that he trusted the stranger.

*　　　*　　　*

"Does he know?"

Ellie had barely removed her coat and sat down at the table in the small restaurant before the questions began.

"No, he doesn't. Though I know he senses that there's something big that I'm not telling him. He's asked me a few times and it's getting harder to not tell him."

"You don't think he would understand?"

Ellie shook her head. "No, that's not it. I know he would understand, because I've told him before."

"In a previous life? You told him?"

Ellie picked up the menu, she was starving. "Yes, I did. And he understood, he was even relieved that I had told him. He was glad he knew."

Elijah picked up his menu. "So was that lifetime better than the others? I still can't quite believe that you have managed to change your life. I never thought it was possible."

Ellie sighed. "No, that life wasn't better. In fact, it was worse. I did change the outcome, but it wasn't for the better. Which is why I decided never to tell him about it again. But then I wasn't planning on him being a totally different man this time either."

Elijah's eyebrows shot up. "*He's* changed? He's not the same?"

"No, he seems to have retained some memory from the previous life and has somehow changed his way of thinking based on that memory. Though he doesn't realise that it was a memory."

The waiter arrived and Ellie ordered eagerly. Elijah just ordered some side dishes. He seemed too distracted to look at the menu properly. He looked up at Ellie and blinked several times. "Just when I think I've got everything figured out, I realise that I haven't a clue how any of this works."

Ellie chuckled. "Tell me about it. I used to be like you, I used to think that I couldn't change anything. It was Mrs M that made me realise otherwise."

"Mrs M? Who was she? Did she remember too?"

"No, she didn't remember, but she was a psychic. She knew that I lived my life over and over, and that I could remember each life. She was the one who told me that I was the only one. Up until then, I just figured that everyone was living their lives repeatedly, but they just didn't remember."

"I must admit, I'd thought the same, though I've never really spoken to anyone about it. But is it really just us? How does that work?"

Ellie sighed. "I only have theories, I don't know for certain. Mrs M didn't seem to know either."

"I'd like to meet this Mrs M. Do you know where I can find her?"

"I'm afraid she died a few years ago."

Elijah sighed. "Well, that is sad."

"I worked with her for a few years, and it took that long for me to properly let go of the past and the possible future and live in the now. Though I still slip up at times."

"Why does it take so long? To let go?"

"Because we see our past as being our identity. We think that we are the sum of our experiences. But we're not. What we have experienced before does not have to have any bearing on what we can experience in the future. If we can just let go of everything else, we can create our futures based on our present thoughts. Which means, of course, that to create a happy future, we need to change our present thoughts to more positive ones.

"What I said earlier, about changing things, was wrong. I didn't change *things*, you cannot change things. What I meant was that I changed *myself*. I changed my thoughts, my beliefs. I stopped thinking about the past and the future, and I trained myself to remain purely in the present. In doing so, I have changed the course of my life."

Just then, their food arrived and Ellie tucked into her risotto with enthusiasm. She looked up after a few mouthfuls and saw that Elijah wasn't eating, but looking at something over her shoulder. "What is it?" she asked.

Elijah frowned. "Is that your boyfriend sitting over there?"

Ellie frowned back and turned around just in time to see Luke bring the menu up in front of his face in an attempt to hide. She turned back to Elijah and shook her head. "See, I told you he suspected something was up. He's more spiritual in this life, more in tune with people's energy. It's really hard to keep anything from him." She sighed. "But I thought he trusted me." She looked around again and this time caught his eye. She smiled and motioned for him to come over.

"If we let him join us, maybe he won't be so suspicious. Just pretend we were talking about spiritual things," she whispered.

"Well, that's no lie. We were."

A second later, Ellie felt a hand on her shoulder. She looked up at Luke and smiled. "Fancied a bite to eat, did you?" she asked innocently.

He shrugged a bit sheepishly. "Just got a bit lonely at home."

"Of course you did. Why don't you grab a chair and join us? Have you ordered?"

Luke frowned. "Are you sure that's okay?"

Ellie stood up and kissed him. "Of course it's okay, silly. Go get a chair."

The relief radiated from him, and he looked at Elijah who quickly nodded his assent. Luke got a chair and joined their table. He ordered some food and then silence fell.

"So, Elijah was asking me what other classes run at the centre, and I mentioned yours. Do you want to tell him a bit more about it?" she asked, before tucking into her food again.

Luke looked slightly perplexed but shrugged and turned

to Elijah. As he launched into a description of his classes, Ellie sighed in relief. It seemed like she had dodged having to tell him the truth, again, but how much longer it would last, she wasn't sure.

*   *   *

"Are you mad at me?" Luke watched Ellie's face closely as he waited for her to respond, but her smile was genuine.

"Of course not. I should have invited you along in the first place, I didn't realise that you would get jealous. Elijah is not my type, you know."

"I wasn't jealous," Luke protested.

Ellie raised an eyebrow but said nothing.

"I wasn't! There was just something about him that I didn't quite trust. I just wanted to be sure you were okay."

Ellie reached up and kissed him, wrapping her arms around his waist. "I love you, Luke. But you know I can take care of myself."

"I know," Luke replied, returning her kiss. "It's just because I love you so much. I couldn't bear the thought of losing you." Luke's heart clenched as he spoke the words. For some reason, he knew exactly what it would feel like to lose her, to know that he would never see her again, and he just couldn't let it happen. But he couldn't stifle her either. She was a free spirit and needed her independence and freedom.

"I'm sorry I crashed your dinner. I should have trusted you more. It won't happen again, I promise."

Ellie pulled away and grinned at him. "Don't worry, if I see Elijah again, I will make sure it's at the meditation centre when you're around, okay?"

Luke nodded, relieved though still slightly perplexed. "What did he want to talk about that was so important anyway?"

Ellie bit her lip then quickly released it. She hesitated just a second too long before answering.

"He's just going through a really tough time at the moment, and he wanted to know how to change his thoughts and his life."

"But he could have asked anyone at the centre those questions, why you?"

Ellie shrugged. "Don't know, I guess he just felt some sort of connection with me."

Luke sighed. He could tell that she wasn't telling him the truth, but he could also sense that she wasn't trying to deceive him maliciously. He pulled her close again. "Would you like a cup of tea?"

He felt her relax in his arms, the tension of her lies draining from her as she realised he was going to stop questioning her.

"Yes, please."

Chapter Ten

Ellie kept to her word, and the next time she met Elijah, they sat in the meditation room in the centre, with Luke just a few rooms away. She really didn't want to make him any more suspicious and part of her wished that she could just not speak to Elijah again, but he was desperate for her to teach him how to change his thinking, so that he could change his life.

They sat cross-legged on the floor opposite each other, breathing deeply and relaxing.

"I've never tried teaching this to anyone before, so I will just have to do it in a similar way to how Mrs M taught me, if that's okay?"

Elijah nodded.

"Okay, so first things first, do you have any recordings, whether audio or written or visual of your past lives?"

"You mean like my diary?"

"Yes."

"Yes, I have loads of diaries, in each lifetime I try to write down everything that happens."

"Anything else?"

"Oh, yeah actually, I have a load of tapes too. I started recording myself talking about things that were going to happen."

"Right, next time, I need you to bring me the diaries and the tapes, okay?"

Elijah nodded. "Sure."

"Are you ready to begin?"

"Actually, I have a question first."

"Go ahead."

"I looked up the word 'Elphite' online last night, but I couldn't find anything. It doesn't seem to exist, so what does it mean? Where did you get it from?"

Ellie smiled. "You won't find it anywhere online. I made it up. When I realised that I might be the only one who was living their life over and over, a word popped into my mind: Elphite. And," she shook her head, "it's going to sound silly, but I thought it summed me up perfectly because it seemed like a cross between 'elephant' and 'elite'."

Elijah smiled. "Because elephants supposedly never forget?"

"And I was most definitely elite. Yes." Ellie blushed. "I told you it was silly."

"It's not silly at all. It's the perfect name. I am an Elphite. Yes, it sounds good."

Ellie straightened her shoulders. "Okay, if you don't have any other questions, from this moment on, all that exists is this moment. If you speak of the past, I will respond with the word 'past' and nothing more. If you speak of the possible future, I will respond with the word 'future' and that will be the end of the conversation. I may even cut you off mid-sentence if I can see where it's going."

"But how is that going to help? Don't you need to know what's going to happen to-"

"Future," Ellie cut in.

Elijah stopped and frowned at her. "I don't get it."

Ellie sighed. "Every thought you think in each moment is creating your experience of the future. Every word you speak is doing the same thing. Therefore, if you speak of what happened to you in a past life, you will create that same thing in this life. You need to let go. You need to stay present in the moment. You need to release everything, *everything* except how you feel in this moment. All your worry, anger, fear – it's all tied to memories of the past or future. Let the memories go, and you let the negativity go, too."

Elijah's face cleared as he began to understand what she meant. "So every time, I've been the one who is recreating my life over and over in the same way, not fate?"

"Exactly. And if you get lost in worry or fear, I want you to stop and ask yourself three questions. Am I alive? Am I awake? Am I loved?"

Elijah repeated the questions out loud, adding a 'yes' after each one.

"Then turn those into positive statements. "I am alive. I am awake. I am loved."

Elijah repeated them after her.

"And so, if those statements are true, then there is nothing to fear in this present moment."

Elijah smiled, and Ellie saw some of the tension he had been holding in his shoulders drain away.

"Shall we do a short meditation now? Let your mind wander, but if you start to get lost in the past, just ask yourself those three questions to bring yourself back to the present moment. I will begin the meditation with a short visualisation."

Elijah nodded and closed his eyes.

"I want you to take three deep, slow breaths."

*   *   *

Luke knew he shouldn't, but she had left it out in plain sight, and he needed answers. Over the last few months, her secret had pushed them further apart, and was pushing her closer to Elijah. He went to the bedroom door and pressed his ear to the gap. He listened intently and could hear her deep breaths of sleep. He pulled the door closed completely, and then returned to the lounge where her diary lay on the coffee table.

He sat on the sofa, waited another few minutes, then when he felt it was safe to, he picked it up and flipped to the first page. He smiled slightly at her loopy cursive, as it seemed to embody her spirit.

He scanned each page, but it became apparent that even her diary was not going to reveal her secrets. Instead of detailing events, it was filled with positive affirmations and thoughts. He flicked forward a few pages and found the paragraph she'd written about her ideal partner. His eyes widened slightly. He fit the description exactly. Uncannily.

He glanced up at the bedroom door. Was she really psychic? She hadn't mentioned her psychic abilities since their first meeting when she'd told him very specific things about his past. Was that the secret? Did she know of something that was going to happen? Is that what Elijah had sensed? He still felt uneasy about their sessions, which had continued in the past few months on a regular basis. But at least he felt better being just down the hall, and that he could sense she was okay.

He flipped to the last few pages in her diary. She didn't appear to write it daily, more when she wanted to add affirmations, but there were a few more recent entries, and he tried to decipher their meaning. They appeared to be harmless enough. She just seemed to be affirming that she was releasing the past and helping others to do the same. The only one that stood out referenced the future.

I create my future, with every thought, word and deed. And I know that only love and joy lies before me.

He knew enough about affirmations to know that people usually used them when there was something that needed sorting out. They would affirm they lived in abundance, when really they were poor; and they would affirm they were in a harmonious relationship even when they weren't in a relationship. So this specific affirmation about the future made him think once more that she had seen something happening. Something she didn't want him to know.

Luke sighed and put Ellie's diary down, careful to place it in the same position it was in originally.

He sat back and rested his head on the back of the sofa, closing his eyes. Should he demand that she tell him? He knew that she thought she was protecting him by not telling him, but in truth, it felt like it was pushing them apart, that she was slipping further away.

He sat up suddenly. Elijah knew. He could tell. The way they had connected to one another, it made sense. Luke got up and went to the kitchen. He felt bad about going into Ellie's handbag, but he had to do something. He found her phone and scrolled through the contacts. Elijah's number was there. Luke quickly sent a text message, asking him to meet at a coffee shop in town. He knew that tricking Elijah into meeting him was deceitful, and hoped that Ellie would forgive him if she found out, but he had to know what was going on.

He scrawled a quick note to Ellie and left it on the counter, then he grabbed his jacket and quietly left the flat.

*　　*　　*

"What are you doing here?"

Luke sat down opposite Elijah in the coffee shop and set his mug on the table. He'd waited in the back until he'd seen Elijah arrive and settle at a table before approaching him.

"It was me that sent you the message, not Ellie."

Elijah raised an eyebrow. "Are you still jealous? Because I swear that nothing is happening between us, she really is just teaching me present moment awareness, nothing else."

Luke smiled. Though he knew that, it was nice to have it re-confirmed. "I know that. I'm not here to warn you away from my girlfriend, I just want to know the truth."

"The truth? I just told you the truth."

"Not that truth. I'm talking about what you and Ellie both know that you're not telling me." Luke saw the flicker of surprise in Elijah's eyes and knew then that he knew what he was talking about.

"I don't talk about the past anymore. Ellie's trained me out of it." Elijah shrugged. "Besides, talking of the past only recreates it in the future and I have no desire to do that."

Luke sighed and took a sip of his coffee. "But you admit there's something that Ellie isn't telling me?"

Elijah sighed too. "Yes, there is. But it's not to hurt you. In fact knowing about it would only ultimately hurt Ellie, from what she's said."

Luke was becoming more confused by the second. He didn't want to hurt Ellie, he couldn't live with himself if he did. But could he live with not knowing?

"You should take some classes with Ellie, she's really quite good at helping you to stay in the present moment. What she is hiding from you has to do with the past and the future. It has nothing to do with this moment. So in this moment, there are no secrets." Elijah sipped his tea and waited for Luke to respond.

Despite his original reservations about the guy, he did have a point. Luke finished his coffee and set his mug down. He knew that Elijah wasn't going to tell him, but if keeping the secret kept Ellie safe, then he wasn't going to argue.

"I'm sorry I brought you here under false pretences."

Elijah shook his head. "Don't worry about it. If I were you, I'd want to know too. But trust me when I say it's best that you don't."

Luke took a deep breath. He couldn't bring himself to say that he trusted Elijah. "Thanks. I'd better get back. I'll see you sometime."

Elijah nodded and Luke got up and left the coffee shop. As he walked down the street back toward his building, he passed a florist, and without even thinking about it, he found himself entering the shop and buying a large bouquet of bright pink gerberas. Then he went to the jewellers and told the owner that he needed a ring.

*   *   *

Ellie had slept in far later than normal and felt peaceful and rested when she awoke. She reached out and realised that she was alone. She hadn't even heard Luke get up. She got up and stretched, then made her way to the bathroom.

While she was in there, she heard the front door open and close. She finished up and went back to the bedroom. She shrugged her dressing gown on and went out to the lounge.

The sight that greeted her stopped her dead.

Luke was right in front of her, on one knee, a bunch of gorgeous pink gerberas in one hand and a small jewellery box in the other.

Ellie was stunned.

"I know we haven't discussed this, and I know it might seem like it's too fast, as we've only been together just over a year, but Ellie, I love you. And in this very moment, I want nothing more than to dedicate the rest of my moments to being with you. Will you marry me?"

A hundred memories of previous proposals flashed through Ellie's mind. This was definitely a new one. Ellie brought herself back to the present and looked at Luke. In that moment there was nothing she wanted more than him.

"Yes."

Chapter Eleven

She was so beautiful. He couldn't believe that the woman heading toward him down the narrow pier had agreed to be his, forever.

The Pacific Ocean breeze swept past them, lightly rustling her hair and her flowing dress, taking with it all his doubts and fears for the future.

He knew that this was right, and that they could deal with anything, as long as they were together.

When she reached the end of the pier where he stood, he couldn't stop himself from reaching out to her and taking hold of her hand. She smiled up at him and they turned to face the minister.

The ceremony was short and sweet, and had been written mostly by themselves, to include their beliefs. After the kiss that sealed their union, they turned to face their witnesses, Elijah, and Luke's oldest friend, Jamie, who clapped and cheered.

Ellie grinned and pulled Luke in for another kiss, while Jamie captured the moment on digital film.

*   *   *

"I could stay here forever," Luke murmured to Ellie later that night. They were on the beach, lying on the sand, watching the stars.

Ellie snuggled up to Luke and sighed happily. "Me too. Let's not bother going back to the UK, let's just live here."

Luke laughed. "Sounds lovely. Let's do it."

Ellie pushed herself up and looked at Luke. "Do you mean that?"

Luke frowned. "No, I thought you were kidding. We couldn't live here."

"Why not? I've got plenty of money, we don't really need to work. Although we could set up a meditation retreat here. I did notice that there wasn't one on the island."

Luke sat up. "You're serious?"

Ellie nodded. "Absolutely. Think about it, we'd be trading in dull weather for glorious sunshine and stunning beaches; we could work for ourselves and at our own pace. It's not like we'd be leaving many people behind. Aside from your parents, I suppose."

Luke shrugged. "I don't think they'd mind, they'd have somewhere to go on holiday."

Ellie smiled. "So will you think about it?"

Luke nodded slowly. "Yeah, why not? Like you said, there's no real reason not to do it, though are you sure we can afford to?"

"Don't worry about the money, that's not a problem."

"Then let's look into it. But for now," Luke leaned down to kiss her, then pulled her back onto the sand. "Let's just enjoy the stars, then go back to the hotel and enjoy the night. Okay, Mrs Whitchurch?"

Ellie giggled at the sound of her new name. "Absolutely, Mr Whitchurch. That sounds good."

*   *   *

"Thank you for inviting me, I really had a great time, and

I wish you both the best. If there's anything I can do to help, you know where I am."

Luke shook Elijah's hand. "Thanks, we really appreciate you coming, you have been a great help. We'll see you in a week when we come back to pack up."

Elijah nodded, but he looked a little sad. Ellie stepped forward to hug him, and he whispered something into her ear. She nodded and stepped back.

Luke put his arm around her, an action which was not lost on Elijah.

"I'll see you in a week, then." Elijah picked up his bag and headed to the taxi waiting outside.

"I'll see you, too, Luke. Fantastic wedding, wish you both the best. Make sure you come see me before you come back here forever, okay?"

Luke hugged his best friend. "Of course, Jamie. Thanks for coming."

He watched his friend follow Elijah out to the taxi, and then turned to Ellie. "What do you feel like doing today, Mrs Whitchurch?"

"How about we look for our new home, Mr Whitchurch?"

"Let's do it."

*   *   *

Within two months, they had moved to the tiny island of Funafuti. They had chosen a property that had extra buildings and land, with the potential to be turned into a meditation centre.

Ellie loved it. Every day she woke up to bright sunshine and a warm breeze flowing through the bedroom window. She had never been so relaxed in her whole life.

She turned over and kissed Luke's sleeping mouth. He

stirred a little, and kissed her back.

"I'm going to get some breakfast," she whispered.

Luke nodded, his eyes still closed. She knew he'd open them when he smelled the food.

She left him in bed and went out to their small kitchen. She prepared pancakes and made a fresh pot of tea. It was easy these days to remain in the present moment. It was a rare occasion for her to have a flashback to any of her many lives. It especially helped that they had no calendars anywhere, and no clocks either. They had been getting up when they awoke and going to bed when they were tired, and had very quickly slipped into a natural rhythm.

Time had lost its meaning now, which was good, because Ellie didn't want to spend this life counting down the minutes until her inevitable end.

Chapter Twelve

"Where has that man gone?" Ellie muttered to herself as she rushed around the cabin, getting it ready for their new guests. They were due to arrive at the airport in just half an hour and Luke was supposed to go and pick them up, but he had gone out earlier and not returned.

She quickly changed the sheets, swept the floor and hung up fresh towels, trying to stay calm, despite the niggling feeling in her stomach that was telling her something was wrong.

She headed back to the house, her arms full of laundry, and sighed with relief when she saw Luke driving up to the house. She went in the back door and started loading the washer with sheets.

"Ellie?"

"I'm in the laundry room!" she called back, not looking up.

"Okay, I'm just going to pick the guests up now, is there anything else we need?"

Ellie finished loading the washer and switched it on. She went out to the front porch and kissed Luke. She shouldn't have doubted that he would be back on time. He seemed to have a built-in time-keeping function, despite the fact that they rarely wore watches.

"No, I think we're good. Just the guests, please."

Luke grinned down at her. "Yes, ma'am. Certainly." He

kissed her nose and walked back to the car. "Oh, and by the way, why don't you get changed into something nice for when they arrive?"

Ellie looked down at her shorts and t-shirt. She looked back up at Luke and shrugged. "Okay. See you in a bit."

Luke drove away, and Ellie went back in the house. She had no idea why Luke had taken a sudden interest in her appearance, he'd never been that bothered before. She went to the bedroom and looked through her wardrobe. She wasn't really the dress-wearing type, but she did have a couple that looked okay on her. She ran her fingers down her wedding dress and smiled. Though it seemed like just yesterday, she figured it must be a few years now since they got married. They didn't bother with celebrating birthdays or their anniversary, preferring to just enjoy every day, every moment.

She changed into a short, floral dress, and ran a brush through her hair. Her tan meant that make-up was fairly pointless; her skin seemed to constantly glow anyway.

She tidied up the bedroom, then moved on to the kitchen. She was doing the washing up when she heard the car coming back up the driveway.

She dried her hands and went out to the front porch to greet them, but the words wouldn't come out.

"Hey, Ellie! You look amazing!"

Ellie couldn't speak as Elijah got out of the car and ran up to her, engulfing her in a hug.

"It's been too long. How are you? I never hear from you."

"I'm sorry," Ellie whispered. "I should have been a better friend."

Elijah laughed. "Don't worry about it. When you're out here, in paradise, the last thing on your mind is writing letters, but still! Six whole years, and not a peep!"

Ellie's eyes widened. "Six years? What do you mean?"

Luke came up to the porch, carrying Elijah's luggage. Jamie was behind him. "Ellie hasn't been keeping track of time. She has no idea what year it is."

"Seriously?" Elijah said. "How did you manage that?"

Ellie shrugged, her mind suddenly whirring. Six years, which meant that she was...

"What's the date?"

"October sixteenth, 2012," Jamie supplied, stepping forward to give Ellie a hug before following Luke into the house.

"But, but," Ellie spluttered.

Elijah squeezed her arm gently. "What is it, Ellie?" he asked quietly, not wanting Luke or Jamie to overhear.

Ellie swallowed and looked up at him. "It's just that, in a hundred lives, I've never made it to thirty. This is the first time."

A smile broke out on Elijah's face and he sighed in relief. "You must be doing something right then."

Ellie nodded, still in shock. "I guess so."

"Come on, let's go inside, or Luke will know something's up. Smile. This is a good thing. It means that you've finally broken the cycle."

"You're right." Ellie shook herself, and came back to the present. "This is a good thing."

They went inside and had a drink. Ellie showed them to the cabin and while they were settling in, she went back to the house.

"Did you realise it had been that long?"

Luke smiled. "Of course. Who takes care of the bookings? Someone has to be vaguely aware of the date, otherwise we wouldn't get any guests."

"I guess it just doesn't feel like it's been six years. The time seems to have flown by. I haven't even noticed what's been going on in the world outside of the island."

Luke shrugged. "That's not a bad thing. We've created our own world. Now, go and get yourself ready, I'll get the guys. We're going out tonight."

"We are?"

"Yes, I've made reservations at the Vaiaku."

"We haven't been there since we got married."

"I know, that's why I thought it was time we went back."

Ellie smiled. "Give me five minutes."

∗   ∗   ∗

Luke was glad that Jamie was capturing this moment on camera, because the look on Ellie's face when she entered the restaurant and saw all the balloons with '30' on them was priceless.

She gasped and her hand flew to her mouth. Luke started off the singing. "Happy birthday to you..."

Everyone in the restaurant joined in and Ellie blushed scarlet. She stood awkwardly in the centre, not used to so much attention. Finally, Luke led her to the table, where a large bouquet of pink gerberas was the centrepiece.

He pulled her chair out and she sat down. He leaned down to kiss her. "Happy birthday, gorgeous."

She shook her head and smiled. "You do know that today is not actually my birthday, right?"

Luke laughed. "Of course, but I couldn't get these two," he gestured to Elijah and Jamie, who was still filming, "to get their asses out here for your actual birthday."

"We should be celebrating your birthday too," Ellie said, frowning.

Luke smiled and shook his head. "I'm not bothered. I celebrate by being with you every day."

Ellie smiled and squeezed his hand, then turned to Elijah and Jamie. "I still can't believe you two are here. You need to fill us in on everything that's been happening in the UK."

Elijah and Jamie looked at each other and Jamie put the camera down.

"To be honest, I wouldn't know where to begin. Six years' worth of news and current events is a lot to fit into one conversation," Elijah said, picking up the menu.

Ellie laughed. "Okay, forget the UK, what's been happening with you?"

Elijah set the menu down. "Ah well, that's a much easier story to tell."

*   *   *

"Are you mad at me?"

Ellie put down the towel she was folding and crossed the room to where Luke was leaning against the door-frame

"What for?" she asked, wrapping her arms around his waist.

"For making you aware of the date. I know you have been blissfully unaware of it all these years."

Ellie laughed. "I suppose I was just avoiding knowing out of fear. I'm not mad at you for telling me. And I appreciate all the trouble you went to. I really enjoyed the meal last night."

Luke pulled her close and breathed in the coconut scent of her hair. "Good. It just felt important to celebrate your thirtieth year. Like it was some kind of landmark."

Ellie nodded into his shoulder. "You're right, it is."

"Oops, am I interrupting?"

Ellie stepped away from Luke and smiled at Elijah.

"Yes, but don't worry, we won't hold it against you," she teased.

Elijah smiled. "I was thinking of going for a walk down the beach. Jamie's wiped out, but I wondered if either of you fancied it."

Ellie looked at Luke, who shook his head. She turned back to Elijah. "I'm up for it. Let me just get some shoes." She kissed Luke then left the room.

Luke and Elijah regarded each other silently for a moment. "You've got a great place here," Elijah said, finally.

Luke nodded. "Yeah, it's getting there. We've been pretty busy with bookings this year."

"That's good. You and Ellie both look really happy."

"We are. We both feel much more relaxed here. The pace is slower, the weather is better."

Elijah nodded. "I can definitely see the benefits. The UK is pretty dreary in comparison."

"Who is pretty dreary in comparison?" Ellie asked, as she came back in the room.

Elijah laughed. "Was just talking about the UK versus your haven here."

"Oh, goodness. I don't think I could cope with the weather there anymore. Far too cold and unpredictable." She kissed Luke again and smiled at him.

Luke smiled back and waved as they left the house.

*   *   *

"It's really rather beautiful here," Elijah remarked as they hit the sand.

Ellie breathed in the salty air and sighed. "I know. I must admit, sometimes I forget to appreciate how lovely it is. I've just got so used to it now. But you're right."

"So you've done it. You've finally broken the cycle. Do you think it was moving to an island on the other side of the world that did it?"

Ellie laughed and shook her head. "I have no idea. I just know that I've never been this old before. I think the oldest I've ever been was..." she thought for a moment. Her memories of her past lives had faded now. "Twenty-eight and a few months, I think."

"And here you are, thirty years old! You know, most women aren't so pleased to hit this age."

"It hasn't really sunk in yet. I've been so oblivious to how much time has passed, that I can't quite get my head around the idea."

"So you never go on the internet then?"

"No, I leave that to Luke. Mostly I just run the meditation centre and retreat, doing the cleaning and tidying and running some classes. And to relax I come out here, or I meditate. My life is really simple. I like it like that."

Elijah smiled and bent down to pick up a shell. "I like the sound of that. Must be easy to stay present?"

"Yes, it is. How are you getting on with staying in the present moment?"

Elijah turned the shell over in his hands, examining it. "I do my best. It's not easy. Often I find myself comparing things to my past lives. But I have started making little changes, to see if things turn out differently."

"How old are you when, well, you know?" Ellie asked softly. It was something she had never asked, because she'd been trying so hard to train him out of thinking about the past, but she was very curious to know.

Elijah frowned. "I've not yet made it past the age of forty."

Ellie stopped and looked at him. "But how old are you

now? I thought you were older than that."

"I'm thirty-nine."

"Oh, Elijah. I'm sorry, I shouldn't have asked. I shouldn't be bringing up the past like this. After all, it goes against everything I tried to teach you-"

"It's okay," Elijah interrupted. "You didn't know. And besides, you've changed your fate, who's to say that I can't change mine?"

Ellie nodded and tried to smile. "You're right. It's absolutely possible." She hugged him, holding him tight. He held her tightly in response. "I'm so glad that we met, and I'm so sorry that I haven't kept in touch."

"I'm glad I met you too. You showed me so much. And you made me feel like I wasn't alone."

Ellie pulled away and looked up at her friend. "Fancy a paddle?"

"A what?"

Ellie kicked her shoes off and ran toward the sea. She splashed in, then turned and motioned for Elijah to join her.

He kicked off his shoes and ran after her. They splashed each other like children, Ellie screaming every time the water hit her face. She was glad that Elijah was laughing and that the earlier mood had been broken, but she couldn't get her thoughts away from the fact that she may well end up losing him soon.

*   *   *

"Did you have fun?" Luke asked dryly, as a very bedraggled Ellie climbed up the porch steps. She shook her head so that her wet hair sprayed him.

Splashes of sea water hit his novel. "I'll take that as a yes."

"It was fun, I haven't messed about in the sea for ages. Made me feel like a child for a while."

Luke smiled. "I'm glad." He returned to his novel and Ellie went inside to get changed. As soon as the door closed behind her, he lowered his book and sighed. He wished he wasn't still jealous of Elijah's friendship with Ellie, but he was. Their lack of contact over the last few years had pleased him, and had confirmed that there really hadn't been anything romantic between them, but still, knowing that they shared a secret that he would never know frustrated him.

After a few minutes, Ellie joined him out on the porch. She sat next to him on the padded seat and leaned on his arm. Her earlier, playful mood seemed to have shifted to a more sombre one.

"You okay?" he asked, looking sideways at her. She nodded, but he saw the sadness in her eyes.

"I just wish that I had kept in touch with Elijah more. I feel like I've been a bad friend, not writing to him or calling him."

"He could have called you, or written."

"I know, but well, men are pretty useless at those things, aren't they?"

"I guess. Has he missed you then?" Luke didn't really want to know the answer, but was trying to appear nonchalant about the whole thing.

"I think so. I don't know. I guess I just feel bad because in the last six years, I haven't really thought about him much."

Luke blinked in relief. That was exactly what he wanted to hear. "I'm sure he understands. Besides, he's here right now. Why not just enjoy spending time with him while he's visiting and just keep in touch with him more often from now on?"

Ellie nodded. "You're right. I can't change the past. But I can change the future."

"Exactly." Luke kissed the top of her head and went back to his novel. Ellie whispered something, but he didn't quite catch it.

"Sorry?"

"Never mind," Ellie murmured. "Was just talking to myself."

*   *   *

"It's been so amazing to see you both, thank you for coming to celebrate my birthday."

"You're welcome, thank you for having us. It's been fun." Jamie kissed Ellie on both cheeks, and he and Luke hugged. Ellie turned to Elijah, who was very quiet.

She stepped forward to hug him. "Everything is going to be okay. You *will* break the cycle. You *have* broken the cycle. You are alive, awake, and very much loved," she whispered into his ear.

Elijah nodded. "Thank you. Knowing that you have done it gives me some hope."

Ellie stepped back and smiled at him. "I promise to keep in touch this time," she said more loudly.

"You better had." Elijah shook Luke's hand, then followed Jamie into the airport.

"Goodbye, Elijah," Ellie called after him, as she felt Luke's arm wrap around her shoulders. Elijah looked back and waved.

Ellie wiped the tears from her eyes before Luke saw them. She didn't want him questioning why she was so upset. She took a deep breath and looked up at him. "Let's go home."

Luke stared at the words on the computer screen, but they refused to make sense to him. He must have read Jamie's e-mail at least five times before he could take it in.

Elijah was dead.

He had died of a brain haemorrhage just two weeks after they had arrived home in the UK. Jamie said that the funeral was going to be in two days. He himself had only found out about it from an article on the news. Apparently Elijah had been driving at the time, and he'd consequently crashed his car on the motorway, causing a fairly major accident. Luckily, no one else had died.

Luke sat back in his chair and rubbed his eyes. How was he going to tell Ellie? He remembered the look on her face when she had watched Elijah leave. Had she known that she would never see him again? Luke wondered yet again about her psychic abilities.

He sighed. There really was no other way than to just tell her. She might want to go to his funeral, in which case, they would need to arrange flights immediately.

He shut down the computer and switched off the monitor. He got up and went out to the kitchen. He found a bottle of vodka that they'd been given as a gift but had never opened. He opened it now and poured himself a shot. He gulped it down and was pouring himself a second when Ellie came in with an armful of washing. She dumped it on the washer and raised an eyebrow at him.

"You do realise it's only three o'clock in the afternoon, right? What's wrong?"

Luke drank the second shot, then poured another ready to give to her. "I'm afraid I have some bad news."

"What is it?"

Luke sighed. "It's Elijah. I'm afraid he's died."

Ellie's eyes widened, but Luke could see in her eyes that she had been expecting this. That she had known it was going to happen. But that it was also still a shock. She shook her head and her face crumpled. Luke set the glass down and stepped forward to hug her. She collapsed into his arms and sobs shook her body.

"I'm so sorry, Ellie. I'm so sorry."

* * *

She had been so sure that he would be able to break the cycle. That he would live past forty, in the same way that she had made it past thirty.

Ellie stared unseeingly at the sea. She stood in the spot where they had played in the waves, unaware of the water lapping her feet.

He had been so scared. She could see it. Was it his fear that had done it? Had he created his death yet again, because he had feared it so much? Ellie sighed. She hated to be so self-centred, but losing Elijah had made her wonder what was going to happen to her. Was she now on borrowed time? Had she really broken the cycle?

She felt his arms encircle her a second after she sensed his presence behind her. She leaned back on him and closed her eyes.

"Are you okay?"

She shook her head. He tightened his grip and the tears began to roll down her cheeks. She tried to rein them in, she tried to stop, because she didn't want Luke to think that she was only upset about Elijah and wonder if there had been something more between them. She wished she could tell Luke the truth, tell him the secret connection that she and Elijah had shared. But she daren't. Until she knew for certain that the cycle had been broken, she needed to keep it to herself.

∗   ∗   ∗

Luke was secretly pleased that Ellie hadn't wanted to attend Elijah's funeral. She said that there was just too much to do, with the bookings they had, and that it was too short notice. But Luke was certain that there was another reason.

He sighed and carried on sweeping the floor of the meditation tent. He tried to clear his mind, but there was something that he couldn't stop thinking about.

He wanted a family. It bothered him that Ellie didn't have any family at all and that his had always been so distant; emotionally before and now in actual miles. He wanted to be a father. To bring up children and to be there for them in the way his mother and father never were. He thought that Ellie would be such a wonderful mother, but he wasn't sure how she felt about children. Amazingly, in all their years together, they'd never discussed having children. Luke wasn't really sure why they hadn't. It had just never felt like the right time before.

He decided to wait until Ellie's grief over Elijah lifted a little, before approaching the subject.

He put the broom away and sat on a cushion in the centre of the meditation tent. He breathed deeply and cleared his mind, and concentrated on sending healing to Ellie.

∗   ∗   ∗

Ellie lay awake in bed, while Luke slept beside her. She'd had trouble sleeping since Elijah had died. Somehow she felt like she may not wake up in the morning.

She sighed softly. It was such a silly thing to think. She'd never died in her sleep before, why would she think it was possible now? She shifted around a little, trying not to disturb Luke. She looked at his sleeping, peaceful face. She knew that he was worried about her. She hadn't been very good at hiding her fear from him, and he could sense it. She couldn't tell him what the problem was, and she hated the idea of him suffering through the pain of losing her yet again.

But she couldn't leave him. Not while she was still alive. She had proved to herself that it wasn't an option.

Ellie breathed in deeply, an idea forming in her mind. Slowly, she slid out from underneath the covers, pausing every time Luke moved.

She managed to get her clothes on and make it to the door before Luke awoke.

"Where are you going?" he asked sleepily.

"There's just something I need to do. I'll be back soon, I promise." Ellie waited for a reply, but instead heard Luke's breathing slow into slumber once more.

She left the bedroom, leaving the door open a fraction. She walked a little quicker to the front door. As quietly as she could, she left the house, and set off down the palm tree lined path toward the beach. She wrapped her arms around herself and shivered. The late night air had a slight chill to it.

She reached the ocean's edge and stopped, just out of reach of the waves. She watched them roll in and out for a few moments, their edges lined in silver moonlight.

"Elijah?" she whispered. "I don't know if you can hear me, if you have already begun your life again, or if you're somewhere in between, if there is an in between." Her words danced away on the breeze and she shivered again. "But I need to say goodbye. I want to be able to think of you, to remember you, but in doing so, I can't move forward. I need to let you go. So," Ellie reached into her pocket, and pulled out the shell that Elijah had picked up on this beach, and then given to her. She had kept it in her pocket, looking at it every now and then.

"Goodbye, Elijah. I really hope your next life works out the way you want it to, and that you remember to stay in the present." She drew her arm back and threw the shell into the sea as hard as she could. It disappeared into the darkness, but she thought she heard a faint splash over the sound of the waves.

She looked up at the moon for a few moments, then turned away and headed back to the house.

When she slid back under the covers, Luke reached out and pulled her close.

"I'm back," she whispered.

*   *   *

It was as though nothing had happened. Ellie had suddenly reverted back to her cheerful, peaceful self, no trace of the grief and despair that had marred the previous couple of weeks.

Luke was a little confused. Had he missed something? He was afraid to ask her what had happened to change her behaviour so dramatically, but he didn't really want to bring up the subject of Elijah's death in case it caused a relapse. So he just waited.

After a few days, it was clear that Ellie was okay, that she had got past her sorrow and seemed to be fully in the present again.

So it was time. Luke had this sense of urgency about having a family. It was strange, but now that the thoughts were in his mind, they grew stronger every minute, and it was all he could think about.

After a long day of painting the cabins, Luke climbed into bed next to Ellie and wrapped his arms around her. He just held her for a while, and tried to figure out how to say what he wanted. After a few minutes, he just decided to say it.

"Ellie," he murmured into her hair. "How do you feel about trying for a baby?" He felt her stiffen in his arms, and her heart thumped against his chest. He could sense confusion and shock emanating from her. She was still for several minutes before she pulled back from him a little, and stared into his eyes.

Luke stared back, and tried to figure out what she was thinking. When she slowly nodded, and began to smile, his heart leapt and he smiled back.

Chapter Thirteen

Motherhood. It wasn't at all what Ellie had imagined. She had never experienced it before, not in any of her hundred lives. It was incredible. Incredibly beautiful and wonderful and awe-inspiring. And incredibly painful and heart-wrenching and tiring at the same time. Within a month of trying, Ellie had become pregnant. But not just with one child. Oh no, she was having *triplets*. The pregnancy had been relatively easy, despite feeling like a hippo for the last three months of it, but the birth had been a nightmare.

Ellie shuddered any time the memory of the birth came to mind, which thankfully, due to her present moment training, wasn't too often. As a result of the complications, Ellie was unable to have any more children, which was fine, three was more than enough.

The weeks and months passed by in a blur of feeding and nappy changing, and Ellie once again became oblivious to the time passing, other than to notice how her babies were growing and developing. It shocked her when Luke mentioned celebrating their first birthday.

"It's been a year already?"

Luke shook his head. "It must be nice, being so unaware of time. Yes, they're a year old on Saturday, two days from now. I thought that we should at least celebrate their birthday, even if we're not bothered about ours."

Ellie shook her head. "I know, you're right, we should,

I just hadn't realised. I mean, I could see them growing every day, but wow, I really didn't realise so much time had gone by."

"It's only a year. Last time you lost six."

Ellie laughed. "Yes, I suppose so."

Just then one of the triplets started crying, but before Ellie could get up, Luke had already jumped up and headed for the door. "Enjoy your cuppa before it goes cold," he said over his shoulder.

Ellie smiled. Luke had taken to being a dad so easily. It amazed her, knowing how cold his own dad and stepmother were, that he had actually become a very caring, sensitive father. He was so amazing with the triplets. He could calm them into a deep sleep within minutes.

Ellie finished her drink, then went to see if Luke had worked his magic again. She stood and watched from the nursery doorway as he rocked Lily in his arms, while Nick and Elizabeth slept peacefully in their cots. Before he noticed her watching, she left and went to their bedroom. She sat on their bed and flipped through an album of photos that she had been putting together of the triplets. Even though it had never been high on her list of priorities, being a mother had now become her whole reason for being.

She smiled at a photo of Luke holding Nick in one arm and Elizabeth in the other. The expression on his face told her that he wouldn't trade it for the world either.

*   *   *

"She's finally asleep," Luke whispered, creeping into their bedroom.

Ellie looked up from her book and smiled at him. "You

do seem to have the magic touch."

"Hmm, took a little longer than usual tonight, I think Lily may be teething."

"They probably all are, Lily's just the one who will make a fuss about it."

Luke chuckled quietly. "She does seem to be the more feisty one." He stepped out of his shorts and slid into bed next to Ellie. He snuggled up to her side and smiled.

"What are you thinking?" Ellie asked.

Luke looked up and found her watching him. "I was just thinking how much I love my family."

Ellie smiled. "I love you, too." She set her book down on the bedside table and slid down until she was lying next to him, his arms wrapped around her. "Luke?"

"Mmmhmm?"

"There's something that I think you should know."

Luke's eyes snapped open and he looked at Ellie, but he couldn't see her face. "Ellie, it's okay, I don't need-"

"No, I want you to know this. I know I've kept it from you for a long time, but I need to tell you now. I feel like I *can* tell you now."

Luke pulled away from her and sat up. Ellie sat up too, and he could finally see her expression. "It's okay, I don't want to hurt you."

Ellie frowned. "Hurt me?"

Luke sighed. "A long time ago, I asked Elijah. I asked him what your secret was, because I knew that he knew what it was. And he told me that if I knew, it would hurt you."

Ellie's eyebrows rose. "You asked Elijah? He never told me that." She sighed and bit her lip, and Luke regretted bringing up Elijah's name. He'd been so careful not to mention him in the last two years.

"I know. It seems he was more trustworthy than I gave

him credit for. But anyway, it's fine, I don't need to know."

"But I want you to know, because I think the cycle has been broken. I don't think it matters now if you know or not."

Luke swallowed. He hadn't thought about her secret in a long time, but he was desperately curious now. He sighed. "Only if you're sure it won't hurt you."

Ellie smiled and stroked the side of his face. "For once in my life, I'm not sure of anything. And I love it. But I've always felt that until you know this, you don't really know me, and that's important to me."

Luke nodded.

Ellie lay back down and laid her head on Luke's chest. "You know when we met, on the train?"

Luke nodded. He remembered that day so clearly. He couldn't believe his luck when she had spoken to him.

"That wasn't the first time we'd met. This isn't my first life with you."

Luke frowned, and waited for her to continue.

"Stop me if I'm not making sense, I've only ever tried explaining this to you once before."

*   *   *

Ellie was sat out on the porch, rocking Nick in her arms while Lily and Elizabeth slept peacefully in the cot next to her. It was quite cool that morning, but she knew she would have to move them inside when the sun got a little stronger.

In that moment, she felt so peaceful, but her mind kept pulling her back to the night she had told Luke everything. It had been such a relief to confess. All these years, it had been bothering her that he didn't know who she truly was. He didn't know why they had such an intense connection, why she knew things about him. She thought about his response. It was different from the way he'd responded last time. But of course, this time, she hadn't tried to avoid meeting him. Instead, she'd actually somehow caused him to be her ideal man. She still wasn't quite sure how that had worked.

She looked up and saw him weeding the flower border along the drive. He'd seemed distracted the last few weeks though, and she couldn't work out what he was thinking. Was he worried that him knowing would cause her death? Or that her time was short because her life didn't normally last this long?

Ellie breathed in deeply and looked down at Nick. He was so beautiful. Ellie could see Luke in his features, in his nose and his mouth. He was also calm and quiet, like Luke was. She looked up at Luke again; he was vigorously pulling weeds out of the ground. He was usually calm, anyway.

Ellie honestly didn't know whether he had a right to be concerned. She had nothing to compare these moments to. For once, her life was completely uncertain, she had no idea what was going to happen the next day, or week, or month. She vaguely recalled her conversation with Luke in their last life, when she told him to enjoy the uncertainty, to enjoy the unknown. Because when life was predictable, it drove you crazy.

She smiled and settled back into the lounger. It seemed like she had finally got her wish. So the only thing she could do was to take her own advice and enjoy the uncertainty.

*   *   *

By the triplets' sixth birthday, Ellie had finally stopped

worrying. She had made it more than nine years past her normal lifespan. Surely that meant that everything was going to be okay now?

She watched her children playing with their friends and smiled. Watching them grow into their own personalities had been amazing. They were each so different. She went out to the kitchen to get their cakes ready, three different cakes to match their different interests, and as she put the candles on top, she felt arms wrap around her waist. She smiled and leaned back.

"They look amazing. You did a great job of them," Luke murmured into her ear.

"Maybe I should have become a baker. I do enjoy making cakes."

"You can do anything you want to. There are no limitations."

"True."

"Speaking of which, I've been thinking recently, about living here."

Ellie frowned and put the candles down, she didn't like the new tone that had entered Luke's voice. She turned to face him. "What about living here?"

"That maybe we shouldn't? That maybe we should move back to the UK?"

Ellie's eyes widened. She hadn't seen that one coming. "Why? What's wrong with living here? Don't you like it?"

Luke shook his head. "No, I love it. I just think that, for the kids, it's a bit limiting. There's not a whole lot to do and there are so few people on the island their age. It just seems a little limiting and unfair to them."

Ellie blinked. She hadn't really thought about it in those terms. But then, time was passing so quickly, to her, they were still her babies. "But they're only six. And they love it here."

"I know, but it would be easier on them if we moved now. They'd adjust easier and quicker at this age than if we wait until they're older."

Ellie was quiet for a moment. Her earlier peaceful mood evaporated as she thought about moving back to the UK. "I'll think about it. Can we just enjoy their birthday for now?" She turned back to the cakes, not waiting for his answer. After a few moments, she heard him leave the kitchen. She stabbed the rest of the candles into the cakes with a little more force than necessary.

She didn't want to move. She didn't want to leave their haven here. They had a successful business, three gorgeous children, and they knew everyone in the community. For once, they actually had friends. They had made connections with people. If they moved back to the UK now, they would lose all of that. They would become nameless faces among the masses who just seemed to exist because they had to, not because they were passionate about life.

Ellie finished the cakes and sighed. She shook herself and resolved to not think about it for the rest of the day. She didn't want to spoil the birthday party. She forced herself to smile and went back into the lounge. She grabbed two of her friends, Flora and Jo, and together they brought the three cakes out, singing Happy Birthday. Ellie sang with enthusiasm, only faltering slightly when she met Luke's eye. He looked upset. She looked away and focused on the triplets, taking in each moment as they blew out their candles and made wishes.

Ellie made a wish with them. She wished they could stay on the island.

*   *   *

"I'm sorry," Luke said to Ellie's back, later that night.

Ellie's shoulders stiffened and Luke reached out to touch her arm. "I shouldn't have sprung the idea on you like that. It's just that I've been thinking about it for a while, and the idea won't go away. It feels right, somehow, going back. Staying here feels-"

"Wrong?" Ellie asked, turning to face him.

"Not wrong, just, limiting. For the kids. At some point, they're going to want to do more, go to more places, meet more people, and they're going to have to leave the island to do that. I just feel it would be better to leave now, as a family, than to stay here and one day lose each of them to other places."

Ellie frowned, and Luke wondered what she was thinking. Was she thinking of her past lives? She hadn't elaborated on how they'd all ended, but Luke knew that this life had been the longest of them all, and it was something of a miracle that she was still here with him now. His fist clenched. The thought of losing her was unbearable. When she'd told him everything, five years before, he'd worried for months afterwards, afraid that by him knowing, she would be taken away from him. That somehow the Gods would not allow it and would punish them both.

His fears had paled and faded now, as the years had passed and they had remained alive and still deeply in love. He hated the distance between them in this moment, but these feelings that they should move had been so strong, he felt he couldn't ignore them any longer.

"Say something," Luke whispered. "What are you thinking?"

Ellie sighed. "I love you. And I understand what you're saying and why, but I just can't imagine living back in the UK. Perhaps one day we will have to make the move, for

the kids' sake, but for now, can we please stay here? I feel...
I feel safe here."

Luke closed his eyes and nodded. He pulled Ellie closer
to him and she snuggled into his chest.

"I love you. And if you think we can make it work, then
we can stay here."

"Thank you."

Chapter Fourteen

"So has he ever mentioned it again?" Jo asked as she helped Ellie peel potatoes.

Ellie shook her head. "No, it's been three years now, and he's not mentioned moving once." She smiled at her friend. "I'm hoping that means that he's given up on the idea."

"Me too. I can't imagine you not being here."

Ellie wiped her hands on a towel and wrapped them in a sideways hug around her friend. "I would miss you, too. I don't think Luke understands how amazing it is for me to have friends."

Jo frowned and picked up the next potato. "I don't quite understand how you never had friends before. I mean, you're not annoying, you're kind, generous, pretty, happy. Why wouldn't people want to be friends with you?"

Ellie giggled and started chopping up the onions. "Thank you. I guess I just didn't want to make connections with people before." The smile faded from her face. "I'd lost everyone I loved, and it hurt so much, that I couldn't bear to lose anyone else. So I kept to myself. Of course, I couldn't have avoided meeting Luke if I tried."

"And why would you? He is so gorgeous," Jo said, spying Ellie's husband outside, playing catch with nine-year-old Lily.

Ellie nodded. "Yes he is. I know now that we were

destined to be together. No matter what."

"I don't know if I believe in destiny," Jo said, putting the potato peelings in the compost bin. "The idea that the events of our lives are beyond our control is just too bizarre a concept. I don't believe in any so-called higher power. I think we get to make our own decisions, we shape our own lives. For example, if I decided to leave Jim tomorrow, and get on a plane and travel the world, I could." Jo shrugged. "Or I could just stay in bed for the rest of my life, or I could just carry on as normal." She started cutting the potatoes. "My life is not pre-destined, I make my own choices."

Ellie nodded. "A long time ago, I wouldn't have been able to agree with you. Now, I do believe that we have some control over our lives. But there are some things that seem to happen no matter what we do. No matter how much we try to avoid them."

Jo frowned. "Like what?"

"Telling you the many examples would just be delving too much into the past, and you know I try to avoid doing that."

"I know, I was just curious. Do you think that you moving back to the UK is pre-destined?"

"I have no idea. To be honest, I have no idea what will even happen tomorrow. And I like that."

"Well, let's hope that he's forgotten about it by now."

Ellie looked out at Luke playing in the garden. "Yes, let's hope so."

∗   ∗   ∗

"Hey, I found this box in the shed. Did you want to keep it?"

Ellie looked up from the plates she was washing. She

saw the box in Luke's hands and her eyes widened. "I'd forgotten all about that box. Leave it there," she gestured to the kitchen table with her head. "I'll have a look through it and sort it out."

Luke put the box on the table then went over to Ellie. He wrapped his arms around her and kissed her neck. "When I'm done in the shed, how about you and I..."

Ellie smiled. "We haven't got time, the kids will be dropped off any minute now."

Luke sighed. "Maybe later then?"

Ellie grabbed the towel and dried her hands, then she turned around and kissed him slowly. "Maybe."

Luke kissed her back, then he released her and left the kitchen.

She watched him go, then shook her head and smiled. Even after more than a decade, there was still some passion left in their relationship. Sometimes, anyway.

Ellie got a pair of scissors from the drawer to slit the brown tape. She thought it was one of the original boxes they'd brought with them from the UK. She opened it up and smiled when she saw her favourite items from childhood. She stroked the fur of her Eeyore soft toy then set him aside and reached back into the box. When she pulled out her old diary, she gasped. Considering her whole life had once revolved around writing her diary, in the last ten years she had forgotten that she had even kept one.

She pulled out a chair and sat down. Though this diary did not hold her memories of her past lives, it did hold all that she had wished for in this life. It would be interesting to see what had actually come true.

She opened the diary and began to read. With each page she turned, her smile became wider.

She was living her ideal life.

"I'm bored!"

"Lily, stop whining. Go and find something to do, or I'll find you some chores to do."

Lily made a face at her mother then stomped off.

Luke looked at Ellie and she shook her head. Luke wondered again how they had managed to produce three such different children.

Lily had become ever more passionate, fiery and opinionated with age. It seemed like she always had to get her own way, otherwise they all paid for it. Elizabeth was the calm, peaceful, problem-solving one, and Nick, well, Nick just kept to himself. Most of the time, you barely knew he was there. He never made a fuss, never got emotional or upset, never bothered anyone. Luke worried that he might be too introverted, and that being on such a tiny island probably didn't help. He could go for weeks without speaking to a soul outside of the family.

Luke went over to Ellie and kissed her. "She'll amuse herself somehow, she always does."

Ellie nodded. Luke could see the stress and worry in her eyes that had developed since they'd had the triplets. His own eyes probably looked the same, as he found it much harder to remain calm, meditate and stay present while being a father. He worried about his kids all the time. He knew that it was silly, that he had to let them grow and to make their own mistakes, but it was hard to stand by and do nothing sometimes.

He watched Ellie do the washing up for a few minutes, then said quietly. "Do you think it might be time now?"

Ellie stopped and looked at him. "Time for what?"

"Time to leave the island. To return to the UK."

Ellie went still and stared at him. "I thought that the

idea of moving was off the table."

Luke shook his head. "No, I thought we were just waiting a while. The triplets are twelve now, and I know that Lily is getting frustrated at the lack of things to do. Nick doesn't even talk to anyone outside the family, which is not right, and I know that Lizzie would want what's best for everyone, so..." Luke stopped talking when he saw Ellie's expression. When a tear slid down her face he stepped forward to hug her.

"I know it's not something you really want, but I just think it's what's best for the kids-"

"You don't think I want what's best for the kids?" Ellie pulled away from Luke and looked up at him. "They're everything to me, you know that I would do anything for them. How can you imply that I would put myself first?"

"That's not what I meant, I just-"

"It doesn't matter what you meant. I don't think that moving to the UK *is* the best thing for them. Not at all." Ellie went back to doing the washing up and ignored Luke.

Luke sighed. He could feel himself getting annoyed and he breathed deeply, trying to remain calm. In twenty years they had never once had an argument. And he really didn't want to begin one now, but he'd waited patiently for years, and he really did think it was time to move.

"Ellie, don't you think we should at least talk about this, as a family? The triplets are old enough to decide what they want for themselves now-"

"They have no idea what the UK is like. They don't know what it's like to live there, how could they possibly make a decision over whether to move there-"

"They're not stupid!" Luke shouted, his temper suddenly flaring. "We can tell them everything they need to make the decision, why won't you at least ask them-"

"I'm not going back!" Ellie screamed, slamming the

plate into the sink hard enough for it to shatter. "Not now, not ever!"

She ran out of the kitchen and Luke slumped against the counter. Why had he lost his temper like that? He never shouted, and neither did Ellie. Not even when the kids were being naughty. They just weren't the shouting kind of family. He debated whether to go after her, to apologise, but his frustration was still simmering and he thought it best that he go and find somewhere quiet to calm down. He went outside. He did really love it here, with the consistently warm weather, and the health benefits of that, but it still didn't erase his worries that it wasn't the best thing for the triplets. Soon they would be teenagers, and Luke knew that Lily already felt the constraints of the island. Elizabeth and Nick were still both very contented but he knew that soon, they too would want to spread their wings a little more. What then?

Luke found Nick sat under a tree on a blanket, reading one of his many books. He always joked that he could open his own library with the amount of books he owned.

He stopped next to him and after a few moments, Nick looked up.

"May I sit with you?"

Nick patted the blanket and Luke settled down next to him. Nick leaned against him slightly, but carried on reading. They often had these quiet moments, and Luke used them to try and still his mind, and to count all the many things in his life he was grateful for. Today, he just tried to regain his sense of calm. He regretted shouting now, it seemed unnecessary and uncalled for. He shouldn't have implied that Ellie didn't want what was best for the kids, she loved them as much as he did.

Slowly, his heartbeat returned to normal, and his frustration melted. He loved Ellie. With his entire being.

And there was nothing that would make him leave her, or force her to do what she didn't want to. She obviously felt quite strongly about not returning to the UK, and perhaps for good reason. Maybe she felt that if they returned it would in some way be going back into an old cycle, one where her life was shorter.

He breathed in the still, humid air. He would tell her they could stay. Maybe they could take trips with the kids to different places. Widen their horizons that way. Luke nodded to himself. Yes, they would work things out.

He breathed in deeply and thanked the universe for bringing him and Ellie together. He felt so lucky to have spent the last twenty years with her. The fact that they still loved each other passionately and enjoyed each other's company seemed like a miracle.

Luke released his worries about the future and relaxed.

Life really didn't get any better than this.

$*$ $*$ $*$

Once Ellie had calmed down, she wondered why Luke had acted like he had. Did he really think that staying here was damaging the triplets? She hated to argue with him, they never shouted at each other like that normally. She breathed in deeply. Maybe he had a point. Maybe they should at least discuss it as a family. She knew that the triplets were capable of making their own decisions.

But maybe they could move somewhere other than the UK. As much as she had tried to let them go, Ellie just had too many bad memories of being there to want to go back. She returned to the kitchen, cleaned up the broken china and finished the washing up. She looked out of the window and saw Luke and Nick in their favourite spot, under a palm tree at the very bottom of the garden. She smiled.

They would make up later. She knew that Luke was probably already regretting their argument by now, too.

She finished sorting out the kitchen and went to start on the bedrooms. Though they tried to get the kids to clean up after themselves, Nick seemed to be the only one who listened.

She opened the door to Lily's room and shook her head. It was in such a state of destruction, Ellie didn't even know where she would begin.

She took a bobble from her pocket and tied her hair up, then she plunged into the chaos. She filled almost an entire bag with rubbish. She shook her head. How on earth could one child produce so much mess?

Over an hour later, the room vaguely resembled a bedroom again, and Ellie staggered out, weighed down by the rubbish that she had cleared. Luckily, aside from a few dirty clothes, Nick and Elizabeth's bedrooms were neat and clean in comparison, so she left them alone.

She put the bin bags outside and flopped onto the front porch. She watched Luke and Nick for a while, seemingly content in each other's company. She didn't want to disturb them. Elizabeth was at her friend's house and would be back later for dinner. She figured Lily must be around somewhere. She usually ended up at the beach, watching the local surfers.

Ellie closed her eyes and leaned sideways against the post. Though she loved her life, she couldn't help but feel a little tired. She seemed to run around all day, every day, just keeping everything clean, everyone fed and everyone else happy. She very rarely just stopped and took time for herself. Maybe that's why she had lost her temper, too. After all, life here was much more laid back compared to the UK. Her life would be far more hectic if they lived there. Ellie sighed and wished she could properly let go of all the things that were bothering her and stay in the present moment. Then perhaps she could work out what was best for her family. It had been such a long time since she'd sat in meditation - they brought teachers in now, for the retreat. All she seemed to do was the cooking, cleaning, and taking care of the kids.

With that thought in her mind, she jumped up, figuring that if everyone was occupied in their own pursuits, then they couldn't be annoyed with her for doing something for herself.

She went inside and got her meditation cushion from underneath the bed. She placed it facing the window, so that the sunlight streamed through onto her face. She sat in the lotus position (though her limbs protested slightly) and closed her eyes. She took three deep breaths, and almost instantly her body relaxed.

First of all, she asked herself the three questions that Mrs M had asked her, so long ago.

"Am I alive? Am I awake? Am I loved?" She breathed in deeply, then released it. "I am alive. I am awake. I am loved." She smiled and thought of all the love she was surrounded with. As she sank peacefully into the stillness, the thought occurred to her that maybe they could move somewhere else. To the States or to somewhere in France or Spain. Hmm, maybe not Spain. Her mind calmed and she stopped thinking and started humming, a low sound that vibrated through her throat and chest.

It was because of her humming that she didn't hear the sound of the engine coming closer.

*   *   *

"Dad?"

Luke opened his eyes and looked at Nick who was

shaking his arm. "What?"

"Can you hear that?"

Luke frowned and looked up over the trees. "Yes, what is it?"

"I don't know, but it sounds like it's getting closer." Nick stood up, and Luke got up with him. He could sense the fear in his son's voice.

"Hey, it's okay. It's probably just one of those gliders with an engine."

Just then, the noise became louder and Luke looked up again, scanning the small area of sky that was visible. His own senses were now prickling and his breath had quickened.

By the time it came into view, he was already running, but he knew he wouldn't reach the house to get Ellie out before the plane hit.

"Go get help," he shouted over his shoulder to Nick. As he ran toward the house, he tried to shout but the words wouldn't come out. It wouldn't have made any difference. Just seconds later, the plane hit the roof of their home, turning the wooden frame building into matchsticks.

Luke kept running, and seconds later, he got to the back door, which was just about intact. He barely registered the smell of gasoline, all he knew was that he had to get to Ellie.

When Luke saw her small body lying lifeless under the wooden beam of the bedroom ceiling, his heart stopped.

"Ellie?" he whispered, staggering through the debris to get to her. He stroked her face. She was so still. With the smell of gasoline getting stronger, Luke knew that whether she was alive or not, he had to get her out of there. He cleared the smaller pieces away from her and found that the beam was pinning her down. Fighting back tears and his fear that it was already too late, Luke channelled all his strength and energy into lifting the heavy wooden beam from his wife.

Once it was clear, he didn't waste another second. He carefully gathered her broken body in his arms and made his way to the back door. Once outside, he ran a few yards away from the house and laid her down gently on the grass.

"Ellie," he whispered, smoothing her hair back from her face. "Please stay with me, Ellie. I love you. Please stay. I'm sorry I shouted at you. Please, please stay with me." He held her wrist, and sighed in relief when he felt a pulse. It was weak, but it was there. He looked back at the house and thought about going to see if anyone from the light aircraft had survived, but a second later, the wreck and his home erupted into flames. He watched the blaze, and even from this distance he could feel the heat. There was no way anyone could survive that.

Nick came running up the driveway, his horrified gaze on the burning building. He looked at Luke, and stopped a few feet away when he saw his mother. His hand over his mouth, tears streamed down his face. "Is she?"

Luke shook her head. "She's still alive, but she's very weak. Is anyone coming?"

Nick nodded quickly and came to kneel next to his mother. He took her hand and stroked it gently. "Mum, it's Nick. Please wake up. Please."

A few minutes later, the island's tiny emergency team came tearing up the driveway, sirens blaring and lights flashing. Luke looked up and saw the shock on the fire captain's face. The paramedics came running over, and quickly got Ellie strapped onto a stretcher and into the back of the ambulance.

"Was there anyone else in the house, Luke?" Peter asked, jogging over to him as the team quickly began to put the flames out.

Luke shook his head. "No, just Ellie. I didn't get a chance to check if anyone survived the crash."

The fire captain shook his head. "Leave that to us. Are you okay?"

"Yeah, I'm fine. Can I go with Ellie?"

"Of course."

"I'll try and get hold of Elizabeth, but if she or Lily comes back, can you tell them we're at the hospital?"

Peter nodded and patted him on the back. "I'll call Jo, she'll bring them to the hospital later. You go look after Ellie now."

Luke nodded and followed Nick to the ambulance. Nick rode in the front while Luke sat with Ellie, and the paramedic hooked her up to a variety of IVs.

He talked to her on the short journey to the hospital, just murmuring words of comfort and reassurance, but she remained unresponsive.

*   *   *

Luke was sat in the waiting room, his head in his hands, Nick by his side, when Elizabeth and Lily came rushing in, Jo just behind them.

"Dad! What happened? The house is destroyed, where's Mum?"

Luke got up and gathered his girls into his arms. "They're taking care of her, but she's very fragile right now," he said quietly. "They won't let us in just yet, but hopefully we'll see her soon."

Lily's eyes were wide. "She's going to be okay, though, isn't she?"

Luke's lip trembled and he shook his head. He looked up at Jo, who had tears running down her face. "I don't know, Lil. I honestly don't know."

"Mr Whitchurch?"

Luke looked up and his stomach lurched at the serious expression on the doctor's face.

"Yes?"

"May I speak to you for a moment in private?"

Luke looked at his kids, the fear on their faces clear. "Just stay here with Jo for a moment, I'll be right back, okay?" They nodded and sat huddled together on the plastic chairs.

Luke followed the doctor down the hall to his office, and sat heavily on the chair that was offered.

The doctor took a deep breath. "I'm very sorry, but I'm afraid that your wife's internal injuries are severe. We've done what we can to stabilise her, but we can only stop the internal bleeding with an operation. Given her weak state, I fear that if we try to operate, she won't make it. But if we don't operate, well, she may have a day or two left, at most."

Luke nodded and tried to swallow the lump in his throat. "What are the odds of her surviving if you operate?"

"About five percent."

The tears started to flow down Luke's face, and he didn't bother to brush them away.

"If we don't operate, there's a small chance that she may regain consciousness, which means that you would have the chance to say goodbye."

Luke looked up at the doctor. "What would you do," he asked hoarsely. "If it were your wife?"

The doctor sighed. "I would say goodbye."

*   *   *

Ellie was confused. Her body felt as though it weighed a ton, and her eyes felt like they were glued shut. She tried to make sense of the sounds she could hear, but they were garbled. She tried to swallow but there was something stuck in her throat.

Finally, after what seemed like a lifetime, she managed to discern one of the sounds. It was someone whispering her name over and over again.

She eventually managed to prise one of her eyes open, and the light nearly blinded her, so she quickly closed it again.

"Ellie?" the tone of the voice changed. "Ellie, can you hear me?"

This time, prepared for the brightness, Ellie opened both eyes a fraction, and focused on the face hovering over her.

"Ellie."

She recognised Luke's voice and tried to smile.

"She's awake, Mum's awake."

She sensed movement, and three more faces appeared in Ellie's field of vision. Her girls. Her boy. Her beautiful triplets.

"Ellie, everything is going to be just fine. We love you so much, you're so beautiful. And I'm so sorry I shouted. I'm sorry I lost my temper. I love you, nothing will ever change that." Luke's voice broke, and Lily moved to the other side of the bed to put her arm around him.

"We love you, Mum, you're amazing," Elizabeth chimed in. Ellie saw the tears streaming down her face and wanted to comfort her, but she couldn't move.

"Thank you for being such a great mother," Nick whispered.

Ellie managed to smile, and tried to tell them that she loved them all too. But she couldn't speak. Her eyes began to close, keeping them open was taking up all of her energy. Before she slipped into oblivion once more, she heard Lily whisper.

"Goodbye, Mum."

∗   ∗   ∗

Luke watched her eyes close and he gripped her hand tightly. Was this it? He couldn't bear for her to leave him now.

"Ellie?" he whispered. He felt Lily's arms tighten around him, and Elizabeth reached across the bed to hold his other hand.

He watched Ellie's face through the blur of his tears and prayed for a miracle that would bring her back to him.

Part Three

Chapter Fifteen

"Ellie? Can you hear me?"

Ellie didn't recognise the voice that was calling her name, and for a moment she couldn't respond.

"Ellie, I need you to blink, or move something to show that you can hear me. Can you do that?"

Ellie managed to lift her index finger on her right hand, but that tiny action exhausted her.

"Yes, she's definitely coming back to us. We'll just take it slowly. Ellie? My name is Dr Timear. If you can just slowly start to come round, start feeling your body again, that would be great."

Ellie remembered that she was in hospital. She wasn't sure what had happened, but she remembered the loud noise and being knocked backwards and hit by something. She remembered coming round once before, and Luke being there with the triplets. She managed to clear her throat.

"Luke?" she whispered.

"Ellie, it's Dr Timear. Do you remember me? Ellie, try to open your eyes."

Ellie swallowed, her throat was rough and dry. She tried again. "Luke?"

"Hmm, she seems to be quite disorientated still."

"Give her some time. She's been through a lot."

Ellie frowned. She didn't recognise the other voice

either, but she was beginning to feel a bit annoyed with them both. Clearly she'd been in an accident and unconscious for a while. And where was Luke? Surely he would have been waiting by her bedside for her to wake up?

There was silence then, disturbed only by the humming noise of machinery and a steady beep. Slowly, Ellie felt more alert, and strength began to return to her limbs. She breathed deeply several times and finally opened her eyes. The light, thankfully, was dim this time. She scanned the room and saw two men in white coats staring back at her.

"Glad you could finally join us, Ellie. How do you feel?"

Ellie began to flex her body, and was amazed that she felt quite good. A little stiff in places, but no aches or pains. She nodded. "Okay. I feel okay. Wasn't I hurt in the accident though?"

The doctors looked at each other. One of them shrugged, then approached the bed. "I am Dr Timear, do you remember me?"

Ellie scanned her memory, not just of her current lifetime, but of the previous ones as well, and drew a blank. She shook her head.

"What year is it?"

Ellie had to think for a while. She wasn't used to taking any notice of the date. She did the calculations quickly. "It's 2024."

"How old are you?"

Ellie had to calculate it again. "Forty-two?"

Dr Timear looked back at the other doctor. "Maybe it'll take a little time to wear off. We should let her rest and come back later."

Ellie frowned. "For what to wear off? Where's Luke?"

Dr Timear looked back at her and smiled, patting her blanket-covered leg. "Don't worry, just take it easy. We'll be back later."

Ellie nodded, now thoroughly confused. Why weren't they answering her questions? Had Luke been hurt too? Where was he? Suddenly exhausted, Ellie closed her eyes and soon fell asleep.

*   *   *

When she opened her eyes again, it was night-time, and there was a woman sat next to her bedside, reading a book.

"Who are you?" Ellie whispered.

The woman looked up and smiled. She put the book aside and leaned forward. "Alex, my name is Dr Memton. Dr Timear asked me to come and chat to you, if that's okay."

Ellie frowned. "Why did you call me Alex?"

Dr Memton shook her head a fraction. "Sorry, I meant Ellie."

Ellie nodded slowly. "Okay. Do you know where Luke is?"

Dr Memton winced. "Ellie, do you know why you are here?"

"Yes, I think something hit the house. I was sitting inside, meditating, then I remember being hit by something, then I woke up in hospital, and Luke and the triplets were there." She looked around the room, but it was empty. "Where are they? Are they coming soon?"

"What else do you remember? Do you remember your other lives?"

Ellie nodded. "Yes, although I have been trying to forget them. Mrs M trained me to stay in the present moment, so that I could create a new life, break the cycle. But I still remember all those lives too. I can't let them go, they're imprinted on my soul." She blinked. "How did you know about my other lives?"

Dr Memton thought for a moment, then sighed. "Ellie, what I am about to tell you, I don't expect you to understand immediately, but I'm sure that in time it will make sense."

Ellie nodded, already confused, and not liking the sound of her words.

"You are not in a hospital on the island of Funafuti. You are in a facility in London."

"London? Were my injuries that serious?" Ellie flexed her toes and her hands, everything felt fine to her. She could feel tubes in her arms hooked up to IVs, but other than that, everything was intact.

"Ellie, you were not injured. You were not in an accident. Your name is not even Ellie. It's Alex."

"What are you talking about?"

Dr Memton sighed again. "Perhaps it's too early to discuss this. It was thought that your memories would have come back to you by now, but then you were under for a while longer than planned."

"But I do remember. I mean, I don't know what you're on about, but I remember my life and who I am." Ellie started breathing heavily, and the machine next to her began beeping more rapidly. "And what do you mean, my name is Alex? I'm Ellie. I always have been."

Dr Memton patted her arm, and she felt a flash of irritation at being treated like a child.

"I'll come back in the morning. Get some more sleep. Hopefully it will be clearer when you wake up."

Ellie tried to calm her breathing and settle back down. "I hope so."

*   *   *

"I don't understand why she can't remember yet, the others always remembered just minutes after awakening, they didn't even need much orientation. Do you think it's because we let her go too far?"

"I don't know. It's an unusual case. We'll just have to see what happens."

Ellie was aware of the voices, but their conversation made little sense to her. She tried to remain still, hoping for them to give more away, but they lapsed into silence.

"Ellie, are you awake?"

Reluctantly, she opened her eyes, and saw Dr Memton smiling at her.

"Good morning, how are you feeling?"

Ellie shrugged. "Fine. A little stiff, but otherwise okay. Is Luke here yet?"

Dr Memton's smile faltered. "Ellie, do you remember what I told you yesterday?"

"Yes, you told me that my name is Alex. That I wasn't injured, and that I'm in London."

"Short-term memory seems to be functioning," Dr Timear murmured. Dr Memton nodded and addressed Ellie again.

"Ellie, I know this seems confusing to you, because it seems that you have retained your memories of being Ellie, rather than your real memories, so I'm going to tell you the truth now, okay?"

"My real memories?" Ellie whispered.

"Ellie, well, Alex, I should say, the year is 2053 and you are twenty-eight years old. You are here as a participant in an experiment. This is not a hospital, but a science lab. We have developed a machine that will allow a person to live several lives within a system. The purpose of the experiment is not important right now. What is important is that you know that your life as Ellie was not real."

Ellie blinked, trying to absorb what she was being told. The words didn't make any sense. "Not real? I don't understand."

"It's a little tricky to explain, but your lives as Ellie were virtual. Essentially, it was like you were a subject within a computer game. Each time you died, we started the game again, changing subtle things to see how you reacted. Interestingly, you never went past your current age of twenty-eight, apart from in the last lifetime. We realise now that perhaps we should have unplugged you from the system sooner. Perhaps then you would be able to remember right now."

Ellie couldn't process all of her words. They were jumbling together in her brain. But something stood out sharply. A question she needed to ask, but daren't. Instead, she whispered. "So all this time, I thought I was fighting fate, but really, it was you? You were deciding what happened to me? Like it was a game?"

Dr Memton looked away. "Not just myself, it was a team that designed the program, and your life choices. Obviously all of the major world events were based on real ones of that time, so they were set in stone."

Ellie shook her head. "So that's why I couldn't change them, why no one listened to me."

"We hope that your memories will return in time, but I must add that you did sign a disclaimer before the experiment, and that you fully understood there was a possibility of complications like this."

Ellie nodded. Dr Memton stood up, and nodded to Dr Timear, who began to make his way to the door.

"Wait." She had to know, even though she had a feeling that she already knew what they were going to say.

"Yes?"

"Was I the only real one? In the system?"

"No, there were other real people there, but you only met one."

"Who was it?" Ellie whispered, hardly daring to hope.

"Elijah. He is an Elphite, like yourself. That's what we called the experiment. All of the Elphites have names beginning with EL."

Ellie's heart thudded. "Luke?"

Dr Memton shook her head, "I'm sorry, Ellie, but Luke isn't real. He was created for the experiment. He doesn't really exist."

*   *   *

When the sedation wore off, Ellie groggily opened her eyes to see someone sitting in the chair beside her bed. She blinked a few times. Then she decided that the conversations she'd had with the doctors must have been a dream, because there was no doubt in her mind now. She was definitely dead.

"Mum?"

The woman at her bedside looked up and smiled. "Hey, you're awake." She leaned forward and touched Ellie's hand.

"How are you feeling, Allie?"

Ellie frowned. "Allie? My name is Ellie. Am I dead?"

Her mother laughed, then suddenly caught herself. "Of course you're not dead, Alex. Don't be silly. You were sedated, that's all. The doctors said you got really upset when they told you the truth."

Ellie's eyes widened. "So you didn't die when I was a teenager?"

Her mother shook her head. "Oh dear, they weren't joking when they said you couldn't remember. Allie, dear, I'm alive, your dad is alive, and your little sister is alive.

Even the cat is still alive, though how, we're not sure."

Ellie blinked. "I have a sister?"

Her mother frowned, worried now. "What have they done to you? What were you thinking? Letting them experiment on you? If you needed money, you should have come and asked us, not sign up to something like this."

"I'm sorry, Mum."

Her mother squeezed her hand. "I love you, Allie. I would do anything for you, you know that, don't you?"

Ellie nodded and tears rolled down her cheeks. Her mother's words brought Luke to mind, and she remembered what the doctor had said the previous night. "I was married, Mum, to this amazing guy called Luke. And we lived on an island and had our own meditation centre, and we had three gorgeous children. Lily, Elizabeth, and Nick." Ellie's face crumpled and she sobbed.

Her mother reached out to her and gathered her in her arms. "Shhh, it's okay. It'll all be okay. Shhh."

"If they don't exist, how can anything be okay?"

*　　　*　　　*

The next day, Ellie sat in Dr Memton's office. Her mother was sitting next to her.

"What I don't understand, Doctor, is how it was possible for Alex to lose her memories? Surely there were safety precautions in place to prevent that from happening?"

Dr Memton sighed. "I understand your anger, Mrs Compton, and yes, there were precautions in place. All of our test subjects retained their memories. Alex has very much been the exception to the rule, and we will do our best to figure out why that is."

Ellie tuned out the conversation, it was of little interest

to her. She didn't want to get her old memories back, she just wanted to see Luke and her kids again.

Her mother was arguing with Dr Memton, so Ellie had to raise her voice to be heard.

"Can I go back?"

Both women turned to look at her. Clearly they had forgotten she was there.

"Go back? What do you mean?" her mother asked.

"Go back to my life as Ellie. Get plugged back into the system."

Dr Memton's eyebrows shot up. "I'm afraid that's not possible. We only use each subject for a certain period of time, and considering your memory problems, plugging you back in would not be advised."

"I don't care what you advise, I want to go back. I want to be Ellie again, and I want to be with Luke. I don't want to live in a world where he doesn't exist."

"Alex,"

"Ellie, my name is Ellie."

Dr Memton sighed. "Ellie, you cannot live in the system forever. You would have to come back to reality eventually, and if it's this difficult for you to re-adjust now, it would be impossible for you to re-adjust after another week."

"Another week? I lived a hundred lives as Ellie."

"Yes, but in reality, our reality, you were in the system for just under a week."

"I don't have to go back for a whole week, but please, let me have one more lifetime? Let me be with Luke one more time?"

Dr Memton shook her head. "I'm sorry, Ellie, another subject has already taken your place. I'm afraid you're just going to have to live in the real world now."

Ellie sighed. "Can I at least see Elijah?"

Dr Memton shook her head. "Elijah is still plugged into the system. We cannot disturb him in the middle of a lifetime. We're not sure what complications that would create."

"When will he be finished?"

"We cannot give out the details of other Elphites, it's part of the confidentiality agreement."

Ellie shook her head. "Could you at least tell him that I asked about him when he wakes up? You can give him my details if he wants to contact me." Her grip on a link to her life as Ellie through Elijah was tenuous, but she was determined to keep it.

Dr Memton nodded slowly. "I can do that, but I will warn you now, most Elphites, when they awaken, don't remember their lives in the system. They wake up as though they have been in a coma, remembering only their actual life. You're the only one who cannot remember."

Ellie swallowed. Elijah might not remember her? She bit her lip. That hurt nearly as much as knowing that Luke and her children were not real. "Can I ask one more thing?"

"Of course."

"What does Elphite mean?"

"Electronic Phantasmagorical Individual Technology."

"Oh, okay." Nothing to do with elephants then, Ellie thought to herself, her cheeks reddening slightly.

"Do you have any other questions?"

She had millions, but she sensed from Dr Memton's tone that she shouldn't ask them. Ellie shook her head.

"I should hope that your company does its best to ensure this doesn't happen again," her mother said. "You should at least warn people in the contract that this is a possibility."

Dr Memton nodded. "We are, don't worry." She stood

up. "I wish you the best, Alex, and I apologise once more. I hope you are able to adjust."

Ellie nodded but didn't speak. Instead, she followed her mother out of the room and down the corridor. When she saw the light through the door ahead, she took a deep breath. What would the world be like beyond these walls?

Chapter Sixteen

The journey home was surreal. Ellie stared at the buildings and cars they passed, amazed at how different this world was to that of the 2020s. She began to hope that perhaps this was the made-up world, that this was the unreality, and that her life with Luke was the real reality. The thought made her smile. Perhaps some time soon, she would really wake up.

"Allie, would you like me to stay for a while?"

Without looking at her mother, who was navigating the car, she shook her head. "No, I'll be fine."

"Are you sure? I mean, I know I don't know everything about your life at the moment, but I could help you to try and remember things."

"I'll be fine, I'll figure it out. Although, what do I do? Do I have a job?" She looked at her mother, who was pressing a few buttons on the touch screen in front of her. Ellie couldn't believe how much cars had changed, there wasn't even a steering wheel anymore.

"Yes, you are a columnist for a magazine. Maybe that's why you did the experiment, so that you could write an article about it? I don't know. I just figured you signed up to it for the money."

"The money? Did I get paid to do it?"

"Oh yes, the pay was quite good, though I'm not sure it is enough compensation for you losing all of your memories. But I had a look at the agreement you signed, and I'm afraid I don't think suing them is an option."

Ellie sighed. "Losing my memories of my life doesn't bother me nearly as much as finding out that Luke and my children aren't real."

Her mother patted her knee. "I know, and I'm sorry that you went through that. I wish there was something I could do to make it better."

Ellie shook her head. "There isn't. I guess I just have to adjust to a world where they don't exist."

An hour and a half later, the car pulled over and neatly parked itself outside of a tall building, which looked like it was made entirely of glass.

"I live here?"

"Yes, number twenty-five seven."

"Do I have a key?" Ellie asked, rummaging through the bag that she had apparently taken with her to the lab.

"No, it uses voice recognition."

"Oh." Ellie stopped rummaging and looked at her mother. It struck her then that she had been so wrapped up in her own drama, that she hadn't stopped to fully appreciate the fact that her mother was alive and here, with her. She leaned forward and hugged her, holding her tight. "I love you, Mum. Thank you for coming to get me, and for helping me."

"I love you too, Alex. Don't hesitate to call me if you need anything, and you're welcome to come and stay whenever you want."

Ellie pulled back and smiled. "Thank you. Say hi to Dad for me. Oh, and to my sister, too."

"Niki."

"My sister is called Niki?"

Her mother nodded. "Yes, didn't I mention that?"

Ellie shook her head. Perhaps she had retained a vague

memory while in the system, to have named one of her children after her sister. She sighed. Thinking about her triplets brought her down.

Her mother patted her hand again, and Ellie got out of the car. She walked to the front door, which opened automatically. She turned back to wave at her mother, but the car was already gone. She walked through the impressive foyer and approached the lift door. There were no buttons. Ellie looked around but there was no one to ask.

"Please state your name."

Ellie jumped at the sound of the voice, then replied, "Um, Ellie Whitchurch?"

Nothing happened. Ellie shook her head. "I mean, Alex Compton?"

The lift door opened, and Ellie stepped inside. As soon as the door closed, it was moving. Ellie had assumed by the number that she would be on the second floor, but a few seconds later, the lift stopped at the twenty-fifth floor. She exited the lift (which had wished her a pleasant day) and headed down the corridor. She came to a stop outside door 25.7 and cleared her throat.

"Um, Alex Compton?" she said, feeling slightly ridiculous. Nothing happened. "Uh, I am home? Open sesame?"

"You need to say your password."

Ellie jumped again, but this time the voice belonged to a real live person, stood behind her, a smile on his face.

"I don't remember my password," she told the stranger, hoping that she wasn't supposed to know who he was, though he did look a little familiar.

"I do. I know I shouldn't, but I've lived next door to you for the last five years, and you're not always very quiet when you come home."

Ellie blushed. "Oh, I'm sorry about that. Um, could you tell me the password?"

Her neighbour frowned. "You really don't remember? It's your boyfriend's name."

Ellie's eyebrows shot up, and her mouth dropped open. "I have a boyfriend?"

"Yes, his name is Peregrine."

"Peregrine?"

The door opened, and Ellie looked at it in surprise. She turned back to the neighbour. "Thank you. What's your name?"

"Jed. It was my pleasure, Alex. Are you sure you're okay? Can I help you with anything else?"

Ellie shook her head. "No, I'll be fine, thank you."

Jed nodded and continued down the hall to the lift. "Well, if you need anything, I'm just next door, knock any time," he called over his shoulder.

Ellie nodded and entered her flat, unsure as to what she would find. It was much more spacious than she'd expected, and as she wandered from room to room, the minimalism of it surprised her. In fact, it gave nothing away about the kind of person she was. There was no art on the walls, no books or ornaments. Everything was neat and tidy and, well, boring. The colours were all very neutral, it could easily have been a show home.

Frustrated, Ellie started opening cupboards and drawers, determined to find clues as to who she was. In the bedroom she went through the bedside table, but found nothing. Ellie sighed and looked around the bare walls. She couldn't believe there wasn't a single clue as to who she was. Perhaps she should have quizzed her neighbour a bit more.

She stood up and crossed the room to another door. She opened it to find an en-suite bathroom. She went to the mirror and blinked in shock. She had forgotten that she was young again, that she was twenty-eight, not forty-two. She stared at her reflection. It still looked the same, just younger, with less wrinkles. She felt like she had gone back in time and that any minute now, Luke would be walking through the door after being in work all-

"Hello?"

Ellie jumped for the third time that day and her heart started pounding. She moved cautiously to the door of the bathroom, and when she peered around the door, she saw a man standing in her bedroom.

"Alex!" He came rushing toward her and she jumped backwards into the bathroom.

"What? Who are you?"

He stopped and frowned. "Alex, it's me, Perry. Why didn't you call? I thought the experiment finished a few days ago, I've been worried!"

"Perry. Peregrine. My boyfriend?"

Perry frowned again. "Yes, of course. Are you okay? You're acting very strange."

Ellie took a moment to look at him, and wondered how they had got together. He didn't look like her type at all. But then again, maybe he was Alex's type. She sighed. "We need to talk."

"Sure, can I have a kiss first?"

Ellie bit her lip and shrugged. Perry leaned forward and kissed her gently. Ellie closed her eyes but all she could see was Luke's face. Kissing Perry felt like cheating, somehow. She pulled back and tried to smile. "I'll put the kettle on."

"Kettle? What's that?"

Ellie stopped short on her way to the kitchen. "It boils water?"

"But you already have boiling water on tap."

"Oh. Maybe you could make the tea then."

Perry passed her and went into the kitchen. He made the tea, and Ellie watched him, taking note of how he had done it, so she could do it herself later. She wondered what else she would have to learn in order to exist in this strange new world.

Once seated in the lounge with a hot mug of tea in her hand, Ellie looked at Perry, unsure where to begin.

"Perry, I don't know how to say this, but, I don't know you. Something went wrong with the experiment, and I've lost all my memories of being Alex."

Perry placed his mug down on the coffee table and frowned. "But you knew I was your boyfriend, and you knew my name."

Ellie explained her encounter with her next door neighbour. "All I can remember are the lives I lived within the system of the experiment. My name was Ellie and I lived a hundred lives, one after the other."

Perry was shaking his head. "You don't remember anything?"

"No, nothing. I didn't know that my mother and father were alive, or that I even had a sister. And my flat has given me absolutely no clues, because there's nothing here." She gestured to the plain walls and lack of possessions.

Perry sighed. "I can help you there." More loudly he said, "Pictures."

Suddenly, the plain, blank walls erupted into life and colour, and Ellie blinked in surprise. They were covered in collages of photographs, art, and words. There were even moving images, silent videos that had captured moments of her life. She set her mug down and stood up. She went closer to the images and stared at them in wonder. Her whole other life was chronicled on the walls. One whole wall was dedicated to her and Perry. There were photos of them together in all different places. They looked so happy. Ellie stroked an image of the both of them on the beach. She swallowed hard. She wished she could remember so that she didn't have to break his heart, but she couldn't make herself love a man she didn't know.

She turned to him, tears already flowing freely down her face.

"Perry," she began.

"Don't say it." He was crying too. "I know that look." He stood up and went over to her. "I love you, Alex, I've loved you ever since the moment I met you. And you love me. We can get through this, I can help you remember. I can help you get back to where we were."

Ellie shook her head. "I'm sorry, Perry, but I'm not Alex anymore. As much as I know she must have loved you, I'm not her. And I just don't see how this can work."

Perry bit his lip. He wiped his face with the back of his hand. "I love you."

"I know. And I'm sorry. Maybe if I remember one day, we could..." Ellie's voice trailed off, and she knew that he wasn't convinced.

He nodded, tears flowing freely down his face. He leaned forward to kiss her on the cheek. "'Bye, Alex. I'll call you soon, okay?"

Ellie watched him leave, unable to respond. Though she had no feelings for Perry, it brought up her grief of losing Luke and her children. She sank to the floor and sobbed.

*   *   *

"Hello?" Ellie whispered into the phone. It had taken her some time to find it after the ringing had roused her from her tear-induced slumber.

She heard the familiar voice and nearly started crying again. "Hey, Mum." She tried to steady her voice. "No, I'm okay, though it would have been nice if you'd warned me about Perry."

She listened to her mother's apologies and slowly circled the room, looking at all of the images of her life. Not one of them brought back any memories. Apparently she had done a lot of travelling, but aside from Perry and her family, there didn't seem to be any pictures of anyone else. No friends. Strange.

"It's okay, Mum. I broke up with him."

Ellie sighed as her mother launched into a lecture on how her memories might come back and how she should have given him a chance.

"How can I be with someone I feel nothing for? I've just spent twenty years with a man I loved deeply. I can't just switch to another guy without a second thought. I need time."

Ellie touched the words on the wall. It was funny how they summed up her feelings at that moment in time. She and Alex must have a few things in common at least.

"I know it wasn't real." A tear slid down Ellie's cheek. "I know it was just an illusion. But the feelings I had, and still have, for Luke, are real. They're real to me. And I need time to get over losing him."

Though Ellie was thrilled that her mother was still alive, and not dead as she had believed, she just wasn't in the mood to listen to her right now.

"I've got to go, Mum, there's someone at the door."

It took another few minutes to get her off the phone. Ellie dropped the handset on the sofa and looked around the room. Unable to look at her previous life any longer, she went back to the bedroom, climbed into bed and pulled the covers over her head.

Chapter Seventeen

Three days later, Ellie's mindless staring out of the window was interrupted by a soft knock at the door. Perry had rung several times, trying to talk her round. She hoped he hadn't come to try again in person. She got up and went to the door, only to find there was no handle. It occurred to her then that she hadn't left the flat since she'd first arrived back. "Um, open?" she said, feeling relieved when the door silently slid open.

"Hey, neighbour, I just thought I'd see how you are." Jed looked at her face more closely, then took in her crumpled attire. "Not great, by the look of things." He held up the bottle of wine he was holding. "Need a drinking partner?"

Ellie tried to smile, but her face crumpled and she started crying. Jed stepped forward to hug her and she clutched onto his shirt. He guided her into the flat, and settled her down on the sofa before heading to the kitchen. Within moments, he had returned with two glasses of wine. He set them down and handed her a handkerchief.

"I saw Perry leaving the other day," Jed said softly. "Do you want to talk about it?"

Ellie blew her nose and stared down at her hands. "I don't know where to start."

"Start wherever you want, I'm in no rush."

She looked up at Jed and smiled. "You're going to think

I'm crazy."

Jed smiled back. "I know you're not." He took a sip of wine and handed her the second glass.

Ellie took the glass, had a tiny sip, then sighed. "Before I start, would you mind clearing the walls?"

Jed looked up at the vibrant display, noticing all of the pictures of Perry. "No pictures."

Ellie looked up and the walls were now blank again, and she nodded. "Thank you. Well, I suppose I should start with what happened during the experiment."

*   *   *

Jed barely heard a word of Alex's story, because the whole time, a voice was shouting in his head – she's single! She's finally single!

He nodded in what felt like the appropriate places, and he did manage to take in some of it; her many lives as Ellie, meeting her soulmate, then finally getting to have a family with him. The story seemed familiar, but he brushed it off. He was an avid reader and a massive film fan and what she was telling him could easily have been similar to the plot of a film or a book. Then she recounted the last week, waking up to reality, finding out that her lives weren't real, that her name wasn't Ellie, and that she was just a columnist taking part in an experiment.

He finished his wine and set his glass on the table. She was crying now and Jed longed to hug her again, but he didn't want to make her feel uncomfortable. Earlier, when he had held her close, he finally felt like he had come home.

Ellie wiped her eyes with his handkerchief and looked at him. "So what do you think? Should I have given Perry a chance? I mean, I think we must have been together for a few years, and we looked happy in the pictures."

Four years and nine months, Jed thought to himself. He still kicked himself for not making a move quicker. He shook his head. "No, I think you made the right choice. From what I saw, as happy as you were at times, you guys did have problems."

Ellie frowned. "We did? How do you know?"

"I live next door remember? Technology may have advanced exponentially, but this building still isn't entirely soundproof."

Ellie blushed. "Sorry." She sighed. "I just felt awful for hurting him like that."

Jed shrugged. "I'm sure he'll be fine. I'm more worried about you right now."

"Me?"

"Yes, you. You haven't left this flat in days, you've lost weight, and you've just lost everything you ever knew."

Ellie nodded at his summary. "I just can't seem to function. Part of me keeps thinking how ridiculous it is, being so torn up over losing a family that didn't exist, but another part of me just keeps hoping that this," she waved her hand at their surroundings, "is the dream, and that I'm in a coma or something right now, and when I wake up, I'll be back on the island, with my husband and my children."

Jed reached out and rubbed her arm. "I can't even imagine what you're going through. But I do know this. You will get through it."

Ellie looked up at him, tears hanging on her eyelashes. "I will?"

"Yes, you will, because I'm going to help you."

"I can't ask you to do that."

"You're not. I'm saying I'm going to. After all, someone needs to show you how the shower works."

Ellie laughed, and the sound made Jed smile. "I'm sorry.

I bet I smell really gross right now, don't I?"

Jed shook his head. "Not at all."

Ellie's eyes narrowed. "Stop being so nice. You can tell me the truth, you know."

"Okay, maybe just a little bit then."

Ellie laughed again, and Jed's heart skipped.

"So would you like to shower before we begin the tutorials on all the modern technology?"

"Yes, please. And maybe after the shower you could help me find my clothes?"

Jed laughed. "Sounds like a plan."

Ellie looked around the room. "I just can't believe how much things have changed. My last memories are of living on an island with very little technology and gadgets. We even boiled water in a kettle on a gas stove!"

Jed laughed with her. "I vaguely remember using those as a kid."

"Are you sure you have time to help me? Surely you must be busy, with work and family?"

Jed shook his head and took their glasses to the kitchen for a refill. "Nope. Work is easy, and I do it from home anyway. And I don't have any family."

He filled their glasses up and hunted around for some food. He found some crisps and put them into a bowl. He put everything on a tray and carried it in.

Ellie looked up and nodded. "I could certainly get used to the service, I must admit!"

Jed chuckled. "It's nice to have some company, to be honest. To not have to drink the whole bottle by myself."

Ellie raised an eyebrow and looked him up and down. "Surely there must be a list of women just waiting to keep you company?"

Jed laughed. "Unfortunately not. I've been single for quite a while now."

"And why is that? Any bad habits or previous record I should know about?"

He shook his head. He tried to think of a reason that wouldn't scare her away. "I guess I just haven't found the right one yet."

"I'm sure you will. You seem like a lovely guy, Jed."

Jed took a sip of wine and grabbed a handful of crisps. This new version of Alex certainly seemed to be more complimentary. He liked it. "Thank you. And may I say, Alex, that you are a beautiful woman."

Ellie blushed. "Please, call me Ellie. Alex just doesn't feel right to me."

"Ellie it is." He lifted his glass up and clinked it on hers. "To new beginnings."

"To new beginnings," Ellie echoed.

*   *   *

A few days later, Ellie sat in front of her computer, her eyes wide. She couldn't quite believe it. For a start, the screen was huge and there was no mouse or keyboard. Though she had used computers a few times in her life as Ellie, she'd never owned one. They hadn't interested her.

Apparently, Alex lived her entire life online. She looked through the files. There were copies of her articles, a diary, hundreds of photo albums, even videos. She found one and told it to play. The voice recognition thing was interesting, but made her feel a little silly. Talking to a machine just felt bizarre.

The video started playing. It seemed it had been made by Perry.

"So tell me, oh wondrous reporter girl, what adventure are you going on now?"

She watched herself giggling, and trying to shoo him

away. "Stop being silly, Perry, this is serious."

"Of course it is! This is it, your big one. The one that will make you famous worldwide!"

Ellie smiled as she watched her former self poke her tongue out at the camera. "You just wait and see. This experiment is going to change everything, and I'm going to be a part of that change."

The video stopped and her smile disappeared. The experiment had changed everything. She had changed so much she didn't even remember who she was.

She hadn't heard from Elijah. He must be out of the experiment by now, but he hadn't called or e-mailed. Perhaps he didn't remember her, like Dr Memton had warned. Which meant that her final link to her lives with Luke was gone.

She stared at the screen for a while, and wondered if she should just wipe everything. Start completely from scratch.

After all, wasn't this exactly what she had once longed for? The opportunity to have a clean slate, without knowing what was going to happen in the future? Mrs M had trained her to remain in the present moment, and had tried to erase all past history and experiences, so that she could create her future from her thoughts and feelings from the moment she was in. She tapped the desk with her fingers as she debated whether to erase everything.

"You have an incoming call."

Ellie jumped at the voice, and focused on the screen to see that it was someone from the magazine calling. "Answer," she said, remembering Jed's tutorial on how it all worked and what commands to use.

The face of a middle-aged woman with a sleek blonde bob and glasses appeared on the screen.

"Alex? Where have you been? We're waiting for your column, are you writing it about that experiment?"

Ellie blinked and suddenly realised that she would be able to see her too. She wished she'd brushed her hair before answering the call.

"Uh, no, the column isn't, um, quite done yet," she lied. "I need a little more time. But I promise," she added, seeing the stormy look on her boss's face, "that it will be worth the wait."

"It had better be, we want it for the next issue. The deadline is next week, and I want to read it first, so get on with it."

The call cut off and the woman disappeared. Ellie swallowed hard. She wasn't sure she knew how to write a column, all she could remember writing were her diaries. Could she pull this off? More importantly, did she want to delve back into her memories and relive her illusionary past?

She got up from her chair and went to the kitchen. She was getting used to the hot water coming from a tap, and all of the many time-saving gadgets. But it all still felt alien to her, like she had truly been dropped here, in the future, from the past. She felt like she had grown up in the 1980s and 90s, not in the 2020s and 30s.

Maybe this was what she needed. It would give her closure to recount her experience. Maybe she could write the piece from the point of view of Ellie Whitchurch in the early 2020s. She could write about her life in that time, about what she learned, what she experienced. She still didn't fully understand the reasons for the experiment, but she did know what she had gained and lost from it, personally.

She took her tea and her weird biscuit-like things (even food had changed) and went back to the computer. She opened the writing file and began to dictate her article.

"My name is Ellie Smith, and I was born on the twenty-fifth of September, 1982."

*   *   *

Jed stood outside Ellie's door for several minutes before getting up the courage to knock. He looked at the flowers he was holding and wondered if they were too much. Even though they had been spending a lot of time together in the last couple of weeks, it was still only as neighbours and friends. He was worried that if he came on too strong, he would push her away.

He took a deep breath, told himself not to be such a wimp, and knocked on the door.

Within moments, she opened it. A smile lit up her face when she saw him.

"Jed!" She saw the flowers and her smile widened. "Have you seen it already?"

Jed paused, confused. "Seen what?"

"My column! Oh, I thought the flowers were to celebrate?"

Jed gave them to her and thought quickly. "Of course they're to celebrate! I haven't seen it but I knew it was coming out today," he lied. He'd completely forgotten about the column. "Does it look good?"

Ellie led the way in, and took the pink gerberas to the kitchen to put them in a vase. She cut off the ends and arranged them in a black vase she'd found under the sink.

"These are gorgeous, how did you know they're my favourite?" She shook her head and waved her hand. "Sorry, silly question. The column looks great. My boss was amazed when she read it. I'm not sure she quite believes that I've forgotten everything, but she loved it. And she loved my new idea too."

"Oh yeah, what's that?"

"To write about life and everyday things, but from the perspective of someone from the past who's never experienced them before."

Jed chuckled. "That's a great idea."

"I figured it would be a good way to learn about the way things are now without looking like I'm crazy."

"You're not crazy," Jed said softly, reaching out to touch her hand on the counter.

She looked down at his hand on hers then looked up at him. Jed pulled his hand away, worried that he'd gone too far.

"You remind me of him sometimes, you know," she said softly.

Jed frowned. "Of who?"

"Luke. I mean, you don't look like him, well, maybe you do, a little. But it's more the things you say and do, the way you act."

Jed swallowed. "Is that a good thing?"

She shrugged again. "I don't miss him as much when you're around."

Jed moved closer to her, slowly.

She looked up at him. "The thing is," she whispered. "I'm not sure I could love anyone as much as I loved him. I know it wasn't real, but it was real to me." She shook her head. "I thought that writing about him would help me to get over him, but it hasn't."

Jed stopped a few inches away. How could he compete with this fictional guy who had stolen her heart? He was clearly perfect, and Ellie felt like she had spent many lifetimes in love with him. Whereas she barely knew Jed. And he certainly wasn't perfect. But he knew how he felt. His heart was hammering in his chest and he imagined what it would be like to kiss her. He took a deep breath.

"Ellie, there's something you need to know."

"What?"

"I'm in love with you."

Ellie took a step back and Jed mentally cursed.

"You're what? But we've only known each other five minutes."

"Technically, I've known you for nearly five years."

"But that wasn't me. If you love Alex, then I'm sorry but-"

"I love *you*. Who you are, deep down. Who you've always been. And spending this time with you these last few weeks has just made me fall even deeper in love with you."

Jed waited for Ellie to respond, hoping that he wasn't pushing her further away with his honesty. She didn't move for several moments as she considered his words.

Finally she looked up at him, and nodded her head fractionally.

Jed took that as a positive and stepped forward. He leaned down and stroked her cheek with his hand. She closed her eyes and he kissed her, softly. When she responded passionately, it took all of his strength not to just pick her up and carry her to the bedroom. After a few minutes, he forced himself to pull away.

"So do you think we could give it a try? Us, together?"

She opened her eyes and smiled at him.

"I'd like that."

Jed stopped himself from dancing around the kitchen and smiled back. "Where's this column of yours, then?"

Chapter Eighteen

Ellie couldn't believe how much had changed in just a few short months. In some ways, this new life just felt like another in a long line of lives that she had lived as Ellie. Though in this lifetime, she didn't have Luke. Her heart still lurched when she thought of him. Of his smile, his hair, his voice, the way he smelled. She still refused to believe that he didn't exist. How could a person generated by a computer be so real? So alive? The new technology that existed blew her mind.

And her children. The pain of giving birth to them, the love she had felt for them as she watched them grow. How could that have been the creation of a computer? Of a scientist?

For the first time since Ellie had woken up, she realised that she needed answers. She had tried contacting Dr Memton and Dr Timear to ask them more questions when she was writing her column, but they'd refused to respond. She went to her computer and settled into the chair. Surely there must be something online about the experiments?

She opened up a search engine and searched for all the terms she could think of that were related to the science lab, but she kept hitting walls. It seemed that they took the privacy of the experiment seriously. She tapped the desk for a moment, then began to search the internet for anything related to her life as Ellie. Surely if it had been real, there must be some evidence out there?

After hours of finding nothing useful, Ellie started researching the new technologies in general. She figured she could always use the information for future columns, even if she didn't find anything that could explain her own situation.

Another hour later, her limbs aching and stiff, she finally gave up and switched off the computer. She got up and wandered around her flat, looking at the new images and quotes that now decorated the walls. Jed had helped her to change them. Jed. She sighed. He had been amazing. He had taught her how to live in this strange new reality and their relationship was deepening every day, but she still felt like she was holding back.

Even though she could find no evidence to suggest that Luke was real, other than her own feelings, letting him go just seemed impossible.

She read one of her favourite quotes from Mrs M on the wall and wished that she could talk to her.

A knock at the door pulled Ellie out of her thoughts and back to the present. She answered the door and smiled at her visitor.

"Niki!" She hugged her sister, who she had slowly been getting to know. "I wasn't expecting you, come on in."

"I'm sorry, I should have called, but I just couldn't wait to tell you my news."

"That's okay, I don't mind," Ellie said, leading her into the lounge. "Would you like a cup of tea?"

"I'd love one, though I think champagne might be more appropriate."

"Champagne? Wow, what's the news?" Ellie sat down on the sofa next to Niki, the tea forgotten.

Niki grinned and silently held out her hand. Ellie took it and her mouth fell open at the size of the rock that adorned her sister's ring finger.

"Oh, Niki! It's gorgeous! Congratulations!" She threw her arms around her sister, and felt, for a moment, the motherly pride and happiness that she would have felt if one of her own girls had got engaged.

"How did he do it? Tell me everything."

As Niki recounted the proposal and outlined the plans for the wedding, Ellie struggled to remain in the present moment. She thought about her own many weddings to Luke. Weirdly, in this life, she had never been married. Perry had never popped the question, and Ellie was glad. Being married to him would have made their break-up far more complicated. As it was, it had taken several weeks for him to finally give up and stop calling her.

"So will you?"

Ellie came back to the moment and blinked. She had no idea what the question was. "Um, yes?"

Niki smiled and threw herself at Ellie. "Thank you! You're the best sister ever!" She pulled back. "Mum told me not to say this, but I like you a lot better as Ellie than as Alex."

Ellie laughed and got up to make the tea. "That's okay, I don't think I would have got on with Alex much either."

"I told Vim that you would agree to be my chief bridesmaid. He doesn't know the new you, and he reckoned you wouldn't agree."

Ellie sighed in relief. At least she hadn't unknowingly agreed to anything too mad. She took the cups of tea in, and some chocolate cake. She set the tray down on the table, and sat back down.

"Well, for what it's worth, I apologise for anything nasty I may have said or done when I was Alex. I hope I didn't hurt you too much."

"Oh, don't be silly. You know I completely forgive you.

I'm just glad that we get on now."

Ellie smiled. "Me too. So when are we going dress shopping?"

*   *   *

"What are you looking for?"

Ellie jumped and spun around to see Jed standing behind her. "You scared me!"

"Sorry," Jed rubbed her shoulder. "I thought you would have heard me come in." He looked up at the giant screen. "So what are you looking for?"

Ellie looked at the map on the screen and sighed. "I was looking for Funafuti."

Jed's eyebrows rose. "Why?"

"Because I just find it too hard to believe that the scientists could have made it up." She waved at the screen. "But it's not there, so I guess they must have."

"Do you still believe it's real? I thought it was just a virtual reality."

Ellie sighed. "It was, or at least, that's what they told me it was."

"Because it's just not possible. No one can live their life over and over."

"I know. It doesn't make sense. I've even done research into time travel, parallel universes, wormholes and quantum physics, but nothing can really explain it."

Jed was quiet for a few moments. "Have you tried doing any searches for Luke?"

"Yes. I searched for his name and I even searched for the kids' names, the meditation centre, even my friends' names, but I got nothing. I tried searching for reports of the plane crash, but there was nothing on that either. And now as you can see, where the island should be, there's nothing but ocean."

Jed sighed. "If any of it did actually happen, and if the island did actually exist, then all of the information was probably lost in the wipeout of 2032."

Ellie frowned. "The wipeout?"

"Yeah there was a major meltdown and much of the information on the internet was lost. All of the information online now is what was reinstated after the wipeout. Small news articles possibly weren't re-done, and only new maps would have been uploaded."

Ellie sighed, and stared at the map. "So I might never be able to find out, then."

"You could try some forums, perhaps see if anyone out there has heard of the island?"

"Do you think I should? That sounds like it would be a mammoth task."

"I think you should do whatever will give you peace. Whatever will give you closure. I just don't want you to get your hopes up only to have them shredded, and besides..."

Ellie turned to look at Jed. "Besides what?"

"Well, let's just say for a minute that Luke is real, and that he's out there, somewhere, right now. If it was in fact a past life, doesn't that mean that he will be in his seventies by now? Nearly thirty years have passed since you would have died."

The realisation struck Ellie like a hammer. That thought hadn't occurred to her. She had the Luke who was in his forties stuck in her mind. She looked back at the map, at the expanse of sea where she thought her home used to be, and wished it would tell her what to do.

After a few minutes, she heard Jed leave the room. She sighed. She couldn't keep hurting him like this. It wasn't fair. He'd been so patient, and so loving, she needed to love him back in the way he deserved.

She switched off the computer, and stood. Somehow, she would find a way to move on.

∗   ∗   ∗

Jed watched her sleeping, and as her eyelids flickered, he wondered what she was dreaming about. Was she dreaming about Luke? About her daughters? Or her son?

After watching her for several minutes, he made his decision. He slid out of the bed, careful not to disturb her, and made his way to her office, grabbing his phone from his jacket pocket on the way. He woke up the computer and opened a search engine. He whispered a few names, and found the phone number he was looking for. He keyed the number into his phone and then sat with his finger hovering over the green button for a while.

Did he really want to do this? If he found out what he suspected to be true, would he tell Ellie? Would he be able to keep such a secret from her?

Before he could talk himself out of it completely, Jed pressed the green button. It didn't ring for long.

When the person answered, Jed closed his eyes.

There was no doubt in his mind now.

∗   ∗   ∗

"I'm giving up."

Jed blinked sleepily at Ellie, across the kitchen. She smiled at him and handed him a cup of tea.

"Giving up what?" he asked, taking the cup and sipping it slowly.

"On looking for Luke. On trying to figure out whether it was real or not. It's time to let it go. Because you're right. If he is real, then he'll be old by now, and that would just be strange. And if I find out for certain that he's not real, then that would ruin all of my memories." Ellie shrugged. "I think it's better to just let it go. I don't need to know."

Jed raised his eyebrows. "You can live with not knowing?"

Ellie nodded and sipped her tea. "I think it's for the best." She looked at Jed. "How come you're so tired this morning?"

Jed shook his head. "Had a little trouble sleeping."

Ellie put her cup down and went over to him. She wrapped her arms around his waist and kissed him. "How about going back to bed for a bit? After all, it is Sunday."

Jed kissed her back. "That's a fantastic idea. I'll meet you there. I just need to check something."

Ellie smiled. "Don't be long."

∗   ∗   ∗

Jed quickly wiped the history on Ellie's computer, erasing all trace of his research and findings from the night before. If she was happy not knowing, then Jed decided that it was best not to tell her the truth.

Chapter Nineteen

"What do you think?"

Ellie blinked at her sister, not comprehending what she had just been asked. "Huh?"

Her sister pirouetted in front of her, the flowing white dress swirling around her ankles. "The dress. I think this is the one."

Ellie focused on the ivory satin, it was a vintage design with a lace bodice. She nodded slowly. "Yes, I like that one too. Turn around again?"

Niki turned again, in pretend slow motion.

"I like the tiny buttons on the back," Ellie said, trying to sound like she was paying attention. "It's not too much, but it has nice details."

"Yep, this is the one," Niki said, looking at herself in the mirror again. "Now all we have to do is find your dress," she said over her shoulder as she headed back to the changing rooms.

Ellie sighed. She wished she could be more enthusiastic about all of the wedding preparations, but in truth, she now understood why she and Luke always did something very simple, very understated, no fuss, just them and a couple of other people. None of their weddings had been extravagant.

Dresses, cakes, invitations, flowers, decorations, cars, entertainment, food, photographers, venues... Ellie looked down at the tablet she held. Its small size was deceiving. Ellie knew it was full of all the information her sister had been collecting and it made her nervous. There was so much to do, and less than a year to do it in.

"So when are you and Jed going to get on with it and get married?" Niki asked as she came back out in her normal clothes.

"Um, we haven't even discussed the possibility, to be honest."

"But you want to have kids, don't you?"

Ellie shrugged. "I don't know. I haven't thought about it."

Niki pulled her to her feet and they went to order the dress. Once the paperwork was done, they left Ivory & Co. and stepped out into the bright sunlight.

"I think you would be a fantastic mother," Niki said, getting her sunglasses out and putting them on before they headed down the street. She linked arms with Ellie, who couldn't respond.

She wanted to say that she *was* a good mother. That she'd had three beautiful children and that they'd turned out just fine. Though Lily's fiery temper could be a problem at times.

But she couldn't say it. She hadn't spoken of her experience in the experiment to anyone since the day she had given up looking for Luke, given up looking for answers. She wanted so much to just remain in the present, to leave the past behind, and not keep rehashing it all, because really, what good did that do?

As they walked down the street, with the sunshine beaming down on them, Ellie just couldn't see anything around her, she couldn't feel the warmth. All she felt was the cold loneliness inside. She missed Luke more than she could bear at times. He was the missing piece to her fractured soul.

Every time she saw someone who resembled him, her heart stopped. Every time she kissed Jed, she imagined it was Luke. Which wasn't fair to Jed, but what could she do? She did love Jed. She wouldn't be with him if she didn't, but she didn't love him in the same way that she loved Luke.

"You're in your own little world again."

Ellie looked at her sister, who was frowning at her. "Sorry, what did you say?"

Niki shook her head. "What's wrong with you today?"

Ellie sighed and pulled her sister toward a café. She needed a chocolate fix. They ordered drinks then sat down at a table near the window. Ellie watched the people walking past for a bit. The buildings in London hadn't seemed to have changed so much. It felt more like she was back in 2012, when she lived in England with Luke. It didn't feel like 2054.

"Are you going to tell me what you're thinking? Or are you just going to sit there sighing and looking out the window?"

"I'm sorry. I don't want to bore you with my problems…"

"Don't be silly. I'm your sister. I'm here to help you. Just like you're here, helping me. Now talk."

Their drinks arrived and Ellie took a sip of her hot chocolate before speaking.

"You're going to think it's mad, but I miss my family."

When Niki looked confused, Ellie added, "My family from my other life. Luke and my kids."

"Still? It's been months since the experiment."

"I know. But I'm still grieving for them, I guess. I just can't accept that they're not real."

"El, they're not. But you are, and this is. I'm real. I'm

your sister, your flesh and blood, and I'm getting married and you are going to be my chief bridesmaid. And if you have any sense, you will marry that hunk of a man of yours before any other woman gets any ideas."

Ellie smiled. "I know, you're right. But what if he's the wrong one? What if there is a Luke out there looking for me?"

"So what? You can't wait forever hoping you might meet your Luke. Right now you have a gorgeous Jed, who adores you, would do anything for you, and who is madly in love with you. If you throw that away, you're nuttier than I thought you were."

"Thank you, darling sister," Ellie said dryly. She sighed. "He does love me. But, well, I just don't think I do. Not in the same way. I mean, not like I love Luke."

Niki slammed her cup down on the table, making Ellie jump.

"He's not real! He's just a very realistic hologram! Get over him already. Jeez, you're like one of those crazy people who fall in love with fictional characters from books or films."

Ellie looked around and saw that people were staring at them. Her sister's outburst had caught the attention of most of other customers in the café. Ellie looked back at her sister, embarrassed by the attention.

"Can you keep it down?"

"Why? I don't care what they think," her sister said, waving her hand in the direction of the gawkers. "I do, however, care that you are wasting your life pining over someone who doesn't exist. And that you are not giving your full attention to the people who love you. Me, Jed, Mum and Dad."

Ellie breathed in deeply. "I promise I will do my best to focus. I know I haven't been fully present for you, but that will change. I am here." She reached across the table and patted her sister's hand. "I love you. Thank you for putting up with me, I know I've been really annoying."

"Yes, you have, but it's okay, I forgive you." She slurped the rest of her hot chocolate then jumped up. "Let's go look at cakes now."

Ellie quickly finished her drink then stood up too, leaving a tip on the table. "I thought we were going to look for my dress?"

"Are you sure you're up to the task?"

Ellie grinned. "Surely it can't be that hard?"

"Let's do it then."

*   *   *

"Do you want a massage?"

Ellie opened one eye and looked at Jed, who was looking down at her with concern. She nodded her head slightly, then rolled over on the bed. She felt Jed settle next to her, and he gently began kneading the knots out of her back and shoulder muscles.

"That's good," Ellie said, muffled against the pillow.

"What did you two get up to today?"

"Just wedding stuff. Niki found her dress. But we searched every shop in London for my dress and found nothing. We're going to have to look somewhere else."

"Is that why you're so tense?"

"Probably. Niki wants the wedding to be perfect. And the level of perfection she is striving for is hard to accomplish in the time scale that we have."

"I think I'd prefer a much simpler wedding. Just you, me, a pretty location, maybe a few friends and family."

Ellie stiffened slightly under his hands and Jed wondered what she was thinking. She stayed quiet, so he decided to change the subject.

"So has it given you plenty of material for your latest piece?"

Ellie relaxed again. "Not really, weddings are just as madly extravagant and expensive now as they ever were, though perhaps with better technology. Did you know that the venue has cameras installed from every angle, so that a 3D video of the whole thing can be created? It's just bizarre."

"Better watch what we say, if our every word is going to be recorded."

"Uh huh."

Jed stopped massaging her back and lay on the bed next to her, stroking her hair.

Ellie turned on her side to face him. "Did you have a good day?"

"Yeah it was alright, got quite a bit of work done. Ellie? "Yes?"

"I love you." Jed watched her face intently, watching her reaction. She bit her lip, and looked away from him.

"I know. And, I... I know that it bothers you that I don't say the words, but, I need more time."

Jed breathed in deeply then kissed her lightly. "Take all the time you need, I'm not going anywhere."

"Thank you."

*　　　*　　　*

Jed looked down at their linked hands and smiled. He squeezed Ellie's hand gently and she looked at him and grinned. Jed turned to watch the bride and groom, both so radiantly happy, and hoped that one day he and Ellie would be standing there in their place.

It had been nearly a year since Jed had told her to take

her time, but Jed hadn't expected it to take so long. He really wanted to move their relationship forward, but Ellie was still holding back. She still hadn't even said that she loved him yet. He told her he loved her every day, but she never returned the sentiment.

He tried not to let it bother him. He knew that deep down, she did love him. But she was still stuck in the past. She was still in love with Luke. Not that she would admit that, of course. She hadn't tried to find him since she decided it was better not to know, but Jed knew that she thought of him often. He could tell by the look on her face. He tried not to feel jealous, but it was difficult.

He thought again, for the thousandth time, about what he knew. He wondered whether he had been right to keep the information from her, whether it was even right to remain in a relationship with her. But he was afraid that the truth would push her away from him. The thought of losing her was too much to bear. His grip on her hand tightened slightly at the thought, and she squeezed back, not understanding the meaning of it.

Despite her holding back and the secret that he had kept from her, Jed felt that their relationship had deepened. It had evolved over time, and he didn't want to wait any longer to take it to the next step.

Jed turned his attention back to the ceremony, it was simple yet striking. Two souls, committing themselves to spending their lifetimes together.

He saw Ellie wipe a tear from the corner of her eye, but pretended not to notice. What was she thinking? Was she thinking about Luke? He knew that they had been married many times over. Was the ceremony reminding her of that? He tried to push the thoughts from his mind. She hadn't mentioned Luke in months, and he wasn't about to bring him up now.

Later, at the reception, Jed stood and held his hand out. "Would you like to dance?"

Ellie looked up at him and smiled. "I would love to."

Swaying to the beat on the dance floor, under the man-made starlight, Jed's heart pounded as he thought about what he wanted to do. It felt right, to move the relationship forward. He didn't want to wait any longer.

Ellie seemed blissfully unaware, and content in his arms.

"Ellie," he whispered, finding the courage from somewhere. He stopped moving and she looked at him.

"Yes?"

He took a deep breath and stepped back from her, then he got down on one knee.

"Will you marry me?"

*   *   *

Ellie stopped breathing.

She glanced around and noticed that everyone had stopped dancing and was now staring at them, waiting expectantly for her answer. Even the music had been paused, and the silence was deafening.

She didn't know what to do. She looked at Jed, this beautiful man who adored her, who loved her, and her heart thudded.

Was it fair? To say yes, to marry him, when her heart still belonged to someone else? He may not exist, and she might have given up looking for him, but she still loved Luke. She swallowed hard. She knew she had to make a decision, she couldn't just close her eyes and wish the situation away.

"Um," she breathed, and everyone leaned in to hear her. "Yes." Before she had uttered the word, she hadn't known what she was going to say. But now, as her heart steadied itself into a normal rhythm and her body relaxed, she knew it was the right answer.

Jed leapt to his feet and picked her up, twirling her in circles while everyone clapped and cheered. Her sister ran over to her and hugged her once her feet touched the ground again. Her parents also rushed over to hug her and congratulate them both.

Jed's hand never left hers as she smiled and accepted everyone's wishes of congratulations and luck.

"I love you," Jed whispered into her ear, as they were dancing once again.

She nodded and smiled at him, then reached up to kiss him on the lips. But she couldn't bring herself to say it back.

*   *   *

"Congratulations!" Niki squealed for the third time, hugging Ellie tightly. "I knew that he would get his act together at some point."

Ellie smiled. "You knew more than me. I had no idea that he was going to propose tonight. I'm sorry if it took the limelight from you, though."

"Don't be silly. I love the fact that we both got to share such big things together today." Niki looked out to the garden where Jed and her new husband were stood talking. "They get on well. We should come over for dinner more often."

"Yeah, you should, we'd like that."

"Are you okay?"

Ellie nodded. "Yes. I suppose I'm just in shock, really. It feels like the last year has gone so fast, it feels a little like getting engaged is too much too quick."

"But you're nearly thirty. If you don't hurry up and get married now, you won't have enough time to have kids."

Ellie shrugged. "Like I said before, I don't know if I want to have kids. It's a pretty painful process, you know."

"I can't wait to have kids. We've already decided to move to a bigger place in the country so we can have a big family."

Ellie's eyes widened. "You've already got it all planned out?"

"Of course. We talk about the future all the time. Don't you talk about it with Jed?"

"Not really. We don't talk much about us, just about things that are happening in the world, our work, family. What we want to do that day-"

"You haven't discussed the future at all?"

"No, that's why I was so shocked when he proposed tonight. I had no idea he was even thinking of marriage."

Niki shook her head. "Honestly, El, you need to get yourself sorted. Your head's so far up in the clouds right now. You need to come back to earth, you need to wake up."

Ellie sighed. She thought of Luke again, for the millionth time. If he did exist, she wondered if he had sat by her bedside, praying that she would wake up. She wished with every particle of her being that she could go to sleep one night, and wake up to find him by her bedside.

She really desperately wanted to wake up.

Chapter Twenty

"Ellie?" Jed called out when he entered her flat. Though they were now engaged, he still saw this as her place. He was hoping that when they got married they could sell their flats and buy something together, something a little bigger.

"In the bedroom," Ellie called back.

"Come out when you're ready."

Jed hurried to get himself into position and when Ellie stepped out of the bedroom, he wished he could have taken a photograph of her face, she looked so shocked. After a second though, Jed began to worry. Her face was so pale, he thought she was going to pass out. He got up and went to her.

"Are you okay?"

Ellie nodded unconvincingly. "Yes, sorry, just déjà vu..."

Jed's eyes widened. Had Luke done exactly what he had just done? Weird.

He held out the small jewellery box. "I hope I didn't pick the same ring," he said jokingly, though he actually was afraid to find out.

Ellie took the box and Jed noticed that her hands were shaking. She opened it and gasped a little. "It's beautiful." She looked up at him and smiled. "And, no, it's not the same."

Jed sighed in relief and took the ring out of the box.

Ellie held out her left hand and he slid it onto her finger. It fit perfectly.

"I love you, Ellie."

She looked down at the pink sapphire that sparkled on her hand and nodded.

"I know," she whispered.

He kissed her and she responded, losing herself in his embrace. She could do this. She could give herself to him completely. And one day, she would be able to tell him that she loved him too.

*   *   *

"It's gorgeous. And so sparkly! I love the colour."

Ellie smiled at Niki, who was gripping her hand, examining the ring from all angles.

"It is an unusual colour. I like it though."

"Have you set a date yet?"

"No, we haven't planned anything at all yet."

Niki sighed. "You do know that some venues are booked for the next two years already? You need to get on and decide where and when as soon as you can, otherwise you might not be able to get married for years."

Ellie shrugged. "It doesn't really matter does it? I mean, we're not up against a deadline of any sort. But it shouldn't take too long to plan, we don't want anything extravagant."

"So you have talked about it then?"

"No, he mentioned something a while back about how he'd rather keep things simple, and to be honest, so would I. Your wedding was beautiful, really, but all of the planning and the expense of it, it's just not what I want."

"Speaking of my wedding! I have the photos here to show you." Niki set her mug down and dug out a small cube from her bag. She placed it on the table and pointed it at the wall. "I should have the 3D video soon, we'll probably invite everyone over to watch it." She pressed the button on the top of the cube and it began to project photos onto the wall.

Ellie watched the images, artfully arranged into a moving slide-show, and smiled when it paused briefly on a photo of her and her sister. She was very glad that in this life she had Niki, who reminded Ellie of her daughters.

She watched the photos in silence, and imagined how it would have felt if she had been watching Lily's wedding. Or Elizabeth's, or Nick's. She would have been so proud. Her beautiful girls would have made such incredible brides. And her son, he would have been a very handsome groom. She tried to imagine what they might have looked like as grown-ups, but already their faces were faded in her memory.

A tear trickled down her cheek, and she wished that she could have had a little longer in that life. To see them grow up. To grow older with Luke. It seemed so cruel that the scientists had taken away her chance to live a long life with her family.

She looked down at the ring on her finger, and a tear fell and hit the pink sapphire, making it sparkle.

She loved Jed. She was sure that she did. She looked up and a photo of them both from the wedding came on the wall. Yes, she did love him.

*   *   *

A few weeks later, Ellie was at her computer, writing about how cars had changed. She had asked Jed to take her out in his later that afternoon, but she wanted to do a little research first. Her column had been going well, which was amazing, since she didn't remember any of her journalism training. She felt lucky that she had been able to keep her job.

She looked down at her hand, and the sapphire sparkled back at her. She sighed. Why couldn't she tell Jed that she loved him? Because she did. She would never have said yes to marrying him if she hadn't felt strongly about him. But she still couldn't let Luke go. If only she could find a way to get some closure.

She'd considered writing him a letter, and then burning it, or doing a meditation to try and free herself of the memory of him. But she just never seemed to find the time.

She took a sip of tea and settled back in her chair. She knew that Jed deserved better. That he deserved to hear her speak those words. But no matter how hard she tried, she just couldn't verbalise her feelings.

Ellie switched the computer on, intending to do her research, but found herself looking at photographs from her sister's wedding instead. It had been a beautiful day.

"You have an incoming call."

Ellie sloshed a bit of tea on her hand. She still couldn't get used to the fact that everything talked. She set her mug down and wiped her hand on her jeans. She smoothed her hair down, but knew she looked presentable, because she never went online looking a mess anymore.

"Answer," she replied.

"Hello, Alex Compton?"

"It's Ellie Compton, actually. My former name is Alex Compton."

"Oh right, okay. Ellie, my name is Dick Peterson and I want to talk to you about your story."

"My story?"

"Yes, I've been following your column, and I came across the original story you wrote a couple of years ago.

The one about the experiment? About how you only remember your life within the system?"

"Okay, what was it you wanted to know?"

"I would like to buy the rights to the story."

"Oh, you'd probably have to speak to my boss at the magazine if you wish to reprint it."

"I don't want to reprint it. I want to make it into a movie."

Ellie's eyes widened, then she remembered that he could see her, and she tried to make her expression neutral. "Oh, I see. Um, well, I would still probably have to speak to my boss about it."

"Sure that's great. I wondered if we could meet to discuss it sometime soon? Can you come to London on Monday? I'd like to discuss the storyline, because I'd love to know what has happened in your life since the experiment."

Ellie found herself nodding before she had even thought it through. "Sure. I'll speak to my boss today, and I'll let you know when I can get there. Where shall we meet?"

"As soon as you let me know you can come, I'll send train tickets and I will meet you at the station."

Ellie nodded again. "I'll send a reply later today."

"Excellent. Thank you for your time, I look forward to meeting you."

His face disappeared, and Ellie sat back in her chair, in a state of shock. He wanted to make a film about her? And her story? This was unbelievable. Part of her was really excited, but the other part was nervous about the idea of seeing her lives played out on the big screen. Before she could talk herself out of it, she called her boss who confirmed that it would be okay and who was far more excited about it than she was. Ellie sent a message to Dick

Peterson confirming that she could make it.

Within minutes the train tickets arrived on her screen and she took another sip of tea.

A couple of hours later, she was still staring blankly at the screen when she heard her name.

"Ellie? Are you ready to go?"

She had forgotten about her driving date with Jed. She took the mug out to the kitchen and went to greet him. He pulled her in close and kissed her. She closed her eyes and lost herself in the moment, enjoying the sensation of his lips on hers, of his arms firmly wrapped around her. She resolved to gain closure as soon as possible, so that she could commit to him in the way they both deserved.

"So are you ready?"

She nodded and went to get her jacket. As they headed out the door, she hooked her arm in his and smiled.

"You'll never guess who called me today."

Chapter Twenty-One

As the scenery rushed by faster than she could process it, Ellie decided that her next piece should be about the way that trains had changed. No longer were they a leisurely ride through the countryside, now they were the fastest mode of transport across the country. She looked away from the blur of greens and greys to the screen on her lap.

Books no longer existed in the way she knew and loved them either. Now, everything was electronic. She had been trying to read a book, but found it too difficult to concentrate on it. She tapped the screen twice and it went blank. She wished it were as easy to blank her mind. She closed her eyes and was trying to remember some mediation techniques, when she heard someone clear their throat.

"May I sit here?"

She nodded her head, her eyes still closed. When the person sat down, the air around her shifted, and a scent that brought back a million memories surrounded her. Her heart stopped and she became still.

It wasn't possible. He didn't exist. He wasn't real. This must be a dream. Ellie breathed in deeply, and a tear formed in the corner of her eye. She was afraid to open her eyes. What if it was him? What if he really did exist? She slowly moved her hand to the side of her leg and pinched hard. Ouch. Okay, she was definitely awake. She forced herself to breathe, and slowly opened her eyes. She stared down at the blank screen, her heart thumping painfully in her chest.

After what seemed like an eternity, she forced herself to look up.

"Luke?" she whispered. It was him. He had the same eyes, the same hair, the same expression, the same scent. He looked like he had when she saw him last, in his forties. She thought she was going to pass out.

"Excuse me? Sorry, did you say something?" He smiled at her, and she struggled to keep her grasp on consciousness.

"Um, yes, um, is your name Luke?"

He frowned, a smile still on his face. "No, my name is Shadow." He rolled his eyes. "I know, it's a stupid name. I've thought about changing it a few times, but never got round to it. What's your name?"

"Ellie," she whispered, still in shock. She must be dreaming right now, surely.

"Nice to meet you, Ellie. Are you just visiting London, or going home?"

Ellie opened her mouth, but nothing came out. She didn't know what to say.

"Are you okay?" Shadow peered at her, and the concern on his face was almost too much for Ellie to bear. "You look very pale, would you like a drink? I have some water." He produced a bottle of water from his bag and handed it to her. She tried to open it, but her hands were shaking too much, so he took it back and opened it for her. She took a few sips and tried to compose herself. She put the lid back on, not wanting to spill it.

Just then, her phone started ringing. She fumbled around in her bag and finally got it out. It was Jed. Her heart thudded. She couldn't answer it.

"Are you going to get that?" Shadow asked.

She shook her head and pressed the screen. In case he tried again, she switched it off.

"Didn't want to speak to him, huh? I know how that feels. I always switch my phone off on these journeys so I can enjoy the calm without the wife nagging me every five minutes."

"Wife?" Ellie sputtered before she could help herself.

"Yeah, I reckon she thinks these trips are for fun instead of for business. But I suppose she is stuck at home with the kids, so I can't blame her for getting annoyed that I get to escape."

"Kids?" Ellie echoed. She blinked at him, unable to process his words.

"Yeah, three of them. Here, I'll show you." He pulled a tablet out of his bag and tapped the screen. It came to life and he quickly found an album titled 'Family'. He pressed play and a slide-show began, showing himself and a woman in various places. The woman bore such a resemblance to Ellie that they could have been sisters.

"That's my wife, Illuisa. I shouldn't moan really, she's quite an amazing woman. We met on a train actually, some years ago."

Ellie's eyes widened when she saw their wedding, it was just the two of them at the end of a pier, with two witnesses, the sun setting behind them on the water. Then the following pictures made her catch her breath. Illuisa heavily pregnant, Illuisa and Shadow, holding three babies. Three.

"Triplets?"

"Yeah, I know. It was a major shock to me, too. But Illuisa coped just fine with it all." The slide-show continued and the babies grew in each one.

"That's my girls, Lilita and Elizita. And my boy,

Niquito." He rolled his eyes again. "I guess I learned from my parents on the mad name thing."

Ellie bit her lip. They looked just like her children, similar names, too. It was like looking at a photograph of her own family. The family that apparently didn't exist. She struggled to control her breathing, not wanting to start hyperventilating.

The slide-show ended, and Shadow slipped the tablet back in his bag. "Sorry, shouldn't have bored you with my family photos. I know they're not very interesting to anyone else."

Ellie shook her head. "No, it's okay," she said, her voice sounding strange to her own ears. "I'm glad you showed me. How old are they now?"

"They're twelve." Shadow shook his head. "No idea where the time has gone, they've grown up so fast."

Ellie bit her lip. "They're beautiful, you must be proud of them."

A smile lit up his face, emphasising the lines at the sides of his eyes and mouth. "Very much so. They're my whole life, my children. I hate it when business takes me too far away from them, but they know how much I love them."

Ellie nodded. "That's good." She tried to breathe normally, and fought the tears that were threatening to fall. He was her Luke. There was no doubt in her mind. Somehow, he existed, and he was living his life with a woman like her. It was as though she had accidentally glimpsed a parallel universe.

"So what about you, are you married?"

Ellie looked up at him, seeing nothing but friendly curiosity. He didn't seem to notice the connection between them. "No, I'm engaged." She held up her left hand for Shadow to see the ring.

"That's good. Is he a good guy?"

"Yes, very much so."

"Do you love him?"

Ellie frowned, wondering why he wanted to know something so personal. Perhaps he felt the connection after all?

"Yes, I do. I didn't expect to fall in love with him, but it happened anyway." Ellie blinked. She had finally said the words aloud. She had never told anyone that she loved Jed.

Shadow smiled. "I'm glad to hear it. To me, there's just no point in being in a relationship if you don't love the other person deeply."

"I agree," Ellie said softly. She looked at him again, trying to read his expression. But she saw no recognition there, no jealousy.

"Oh, I think we're here."

Ellie looked out of the window, and saw that the scenery was becoming less blurred as the train slowed. Shadow stood and picked up his bag. "It was lovely to meet you, Ellie. I hope you have a good time in London."

Ellie nodded and looked up at Shadow, knowing that this was her opportunity to gain some closure. To finally move on, and let Luke go. "Thank you. It was lovely to meet you, too. I wish you all the best."

"You too, 'bye." Shadow turned away and left the carriage.

"Goodbye, Luke," Ellie whispered. She slumped down in her seat, in a state of shock.

So he did exist. Her gut feeling had been right. But she would never have found him, not with a name like that. It amazed her that somehow fate had brought them together in this moment. Not scientists this time, but actual fate. Though it seemed that they were not fated to be together. She remembered then, Luke chasing her from the train to her home in Spain, and smiled. Yes, she could have followed him this time. But there was no way that she could be the one who broke up such a beautiful family. And it was time to let go. It was time to move on.

She sat there until the train had come to a stop and most of the people had exited, then she picked up her bag and left the carriage. She switched on her phone to find ten missed call alerts. She quickly pressed the screen to call Jed back, suddenly desperate to hear his voice.

"Hey, it's me. I'm sorry I missed your calls, I must have switched my phone off by accident." She listened to his voice and became calm again. "I'm fine, just arrived in London. I'll ring you later to let you know how it's going." She looked up and saw Dick Peterson waiting for her at the the end of the platform.

"I have to go." She paused. "I love you."

She smiled when she heard him say the words back to her. She ended the call, then took a deep breath and headed toward the film director. If he thought her story was an interesting one so far, he wasn't going to believe the new twist in her tale.

Epilogue

"Dad? How are you?"

Luke smiled into the phone, though he knew that Lily couldn't see him. "I'm fine. How are things with you, and the kids?"

"They're good, Elliot is loving school. And Lumie is as mad as ever. They miss you. I miss you."

Luke sighed. "I miss you too. I know it's been too long since I came to visit, but, well-"

"I know, Dad. It's a long way to come. But we would love to have you here, whenever you want to visit."

"Thanks. It's just so expensive to fly these days. And besides, I'm not as young as I once was, you know."

"Young enough to have a life though. I hope you're not in a tiny village surrounded by old people."

Luke laughed. She had summed up the tiny Spanish village perfectly. "I have a great life here. It's not as warm as it was on the island, but it's warmer than the UK."

"I bet it's warmer here in California."

"Maybe."

"Have you heard from Nick at all?"

Luke sighed and looked at the photograph on his desk of his three children. "No. I haven't. I don't even know if he would know how to find me at this point. With the island gone and all of the information online wiped out, it would be a miracle if he managed to find us now."

"I looked for him too, but I didn't find anything. He must have changed his name or something."

"Most likely. He made it quite clear when he left that he didn't intend to speak to any of us again." Luke rubbed his eyes, trying to ward off the tears that threatened.

"I don't know how he could blame you for what happened. It wasn't your fault, what happened to Mum."

Luke sighed. "I know. But I understand. He missed her. I do too."

"We all do. But that's no reason to be like that, I-"

"Lily, I'm sorry, I need to go now. I have an appointment in ten minutes." It was a lie, but he couldn't continue the conversation with tears running down his face. And once Lily got onto the subject of her brother deserting them, it was hard to get her to stop.

"Okay, Dad. I love you. I'll call again soon. And remember, you're welcome here any time."

"I love you too, Lil. Goodbye."

*   *   *

When the phone rang again just five minutes later, Luke wondered whether to answer it. With a sigh, he picked up the phone just before the voicemail service cut in. "Hello?"

"Hey, Dad, it's me." His heart stopped for a second and he thought that Lily had rung back to try again, but then he smiled when he recognised it as Elizabeth's voice. "Hey, how's things?" he asked, settling onto the sofa.

"Have you been to the cinema recently?"

"No, I haven't been to see a film in years, why?"

"Well, Byrney and I went last night, and the main character reminded me of Mum. And the ending, well, it was exactly what happened to her. It's mad, I know, because it was a Sci-Fi thing, with a weird story about multiple lives and experiments, but I swear, Dad, it was just spooky, the similarities."

Luke's heart started thumping. "Did you say multiple lives?" He had never told the children about what his wife had told him about having lived a hundred lives.

"Yes, the main character lives her life over and over, but tries to change things each time. Then she finally gets to live longer and she has a family, but then she's killed in an accident, just like Mum's."

"What's it called? The film?" Luke asked, moving to his desk to get a pen and paper.

"The Elphite."

Luke dropped the pen. That was what she had called herself. He couldn't speak.

"Dad? Are you there?"

"Uh, yeah, uh, sorry, I just..."

"Are you okay? Maybe I shouldn't have told you, I didn't mean to upset you."

"No, it's okay, you haven't upset me. I'm just going to look up this film and see what you mean. It does seem like quite a coincidence."

"Are you sure you're okay?"

"Yes, absolutely. Don't worry about me. I'll be fine."

"Okay, Dad, if you're sure. I better go, I need to get back to work. I love you."

"Love you, too." Luke hung up, then sat and stared at the phone for what seemed like an age. He switched on his ancient computer and clicked on the web browser. Usually it met his needs, but he was impatient with its slowness today.

He went to a search engine and typed in 'The Elphite'. The very first link on the page led him to the film's website. He clicked on it, and there was a trailer on the front page. He pressed play.

"What if you lived your life over and over again? Would you change it?" The voice-over began and clips from the film played out on his small screen. He gasped when he saw the characters. They meet on a train, fall in love, and get married, over and over, until she tries to change their meeting…

It was them. It was based on himself and his wife. But how was this possible? The trailer ended and he quickly clicked on all of the links on the website, looking for more information. Finally, he found a small piece in the section on the director, Dick Peterson, which mentioned that it was based on a story he'd read in a magazine.

Luke searched the internet and found the column in the magazine. When he saw the first line, he nearly passed out. "Ellie," he whispered. "Is that really you?"

Hands shaking, he read the article and couldn't believe it. It recounted everything. Everything Ellie had told him, over forty years before, was there. But he soon realised that back then she had not told him all of the details. When he read the part about her dying in Spain, after he'd left her, he started sobbing. He clutched his chest and blinked away the tears, determined to continue reading. By the time he'd got to the part where she had died in the plane crash, then had woken up to be told it had all been an experiment and that none of it had been real; he was in shock.

How could she think it hadn't been real? That he didn't exist? That the triplets didn't exist? His indignation halted his tears. How dare those scientists take away what they'd had? He stood up suddenly, he was going to set things straight. He needed to speak to her. To this new incarnation of his beloved wife. He needed her to know that he was real, that he was alive. And that her children were real.

He picked up the phone and rang his travel agents. "I

need a ticket to London, England, please. I need to fly there as soon as possible."

*   *   *

He settled into the seat on the plane and knew that in just a few hours, he would be back in his home country. He had done some research and had found that Ellie now lived in London, in a house in Greenwich Village. He hadn't contacted her, he wanted to see her in person. It would just be too much of a shock to explain it all over the phone.

He tried to sleep on the short flight, but found that he couldn't shut his mind down. How would she react? After all, she would only be in her thirties, and he was in his seventies. Would she even want to meet him?

He tried to push away his fears, and focus on the fact that in just a few hours, he would see his darling Ellie again.

*   *   *

"Jed, are you ready?" Ellie called. "We're going to be late!"

Jed came thundering down the stairs. "Okay, okay, I'm ready. Calm down, we're not going to be late."

Ellie smiled and kissed him on the nose. "I'm sorry, I'm just nervous, that's all."

"There's no need to be nervous, it's going to go just fine."

Ellie smiled. "I love you."

"I love you, too, now let's get going. We don't want to be late." Jed winked and jumped away before she could hit him. They stepped out of the front door, and the heavens opened.

"Hang on, I'd better get an umbrella. Can't turn up

looking like a drowned rat."

Ellie dashed back inside and grabbed a black umbrella. As she opened it, she looked up and saw a man looking at her from across the street. She frowned. He looked familiar. She locked the front door and looked up again, but he had gone. Shaking her head, she handed the umbrella to Jed and they set off down the street.

*   *   *

Luke leaned against the side of the building, breathing heavily. He had seen her. And he was certain she'd seen him. Even from this distance, he recognised her. Had she recognised him? But she was with someone and she looked happy. Did he really want to speak to her, to tell her who he was? She had clearly moved on. He stayed there until he was certain that they would be too far away to see him, then he stepped out into the rain, and hailed a taxi.

"Where to?"

"Nearest cinema, please." The words were out of his mouth before he'd even thought it through. But it made sense. He needed to see the film. That would help him to decide what to do. Of course, it would be pretty silly to come all this way just to watch a film. But he could always visit Elizabeth, too. She lived in southern England. He knew she'd like that.

The taxi driver pulled up outside the cinema and Luke paid him before stepping out into the downpour. His clothes weren't really suitable for this weather and he hoped that it was a bit warmer inside, so that he could dry off. He made his way to the counter and purchased his ticket, not quite believing how expensive it had become. He looked down at the tiny square card, and his stomach lurched. Was he really about to watch his own life on the big screen? It seemed like a completely bizarre concept.

Being the middle of a weekday, he had nearly the whole place to himself. He settled in the centre row, halfway back, and watched the adverts and trailers without paying them much attention.

When the film finally began, he took a deep breath.

*　　*　　*

"Excuse me, sir, are you okay?"

Luke looked up to see a girl looking at him in concern. She was holding a bin bag. He looked around him and came back to the present. He was still in the cinema, and the screen was now blank.

"Uh, yes, yes, I'm fine, thank you."

He stood up and his limbs protested. He'd barely been in the UK for a day and already he could feel the damp in his bones.

The girl nodded but she didn't look too convinced. "Do you need any help?"

Luke shook his head and rubbed his eyes. He realised then that his face was wet with tears. He hadn't even noticed that he'd been crying. He pulled a handkerchief out and wiped his face. He then left the cinema as quickly as he was able. Outside, the rain had slowed to a drizzle. He stood on the pavement, trying to decide what to do.

Watching his life, his lives, he corrected himself, being played out on the big screen was so weird. To see himself from Ellie's point of view was even stranger. He didn't feel like the hero that he had just watched. He felt like an old man. Would Ellie really want to know him now? And who was the young man she'd met on the train at the end? Was he another version of Luke? That's what the film seemed to imply.

Multiple lives, experiments, parallel universes. Luke shook his head and the water droplets sprayed around him. It was beyond him. He really didn't know what to make of any of it. But he did know one thing. The miracle he had prayed for, thirty years before at Ellie's hospital bedside, had finally come true. She had finally come back to him. But she wasn't his anymore.

The rain soaked his shirt right through again, but he didn't feel it. He really didn't know what to do now.

"Sir? Would you like me to call you a taxi?"

Luke looked around to see the young girl again, calling from the cinema door. He shook his head. "No, thank you, I'll catch one now."

The girl nodded and went back inside.

Luke stepped closer to the road and held his hand out. A few minutes later, he got into a taxi.

"Where to?"

"The train station, please."

"Any particular one?" the taxi driver asked sarcastically.

"King's Cross, please." Luke had left his small amount of luggage in a locker there. He would retrieve it and get straight on a train to see Elizabeth. Then he would go home. Miracle or not, he could see that coming to London had been a foolish whim. The woman he had seen today was no longer his wife, she wouldn't want to know him now. He was an old man. She was young and had moved on.

He twisted the ring on his left hand. He'd never stopped wearing it, not even after all these years. His heart would never belong to another. Only to Ellie.

He shivered, suddenly feeling the cold of his wet clothing. He wished he had a jacket. A while later, the taxi driver pulled up in front of the station and Luke got out. Lost in his own thoughts, he stepped out into the street without looking.

*   *   *

"What is it?" Ellie asked. She looked past Jed to see all of the blue flashing lights just outside the station. "Has there been an accident?"

"I'm not sure. It looks like the emergency services are there though."

As they walked past, Ellie saw someone lying in the street, and paramedics tending to him. When she saw his clothes, she frowned. She could have sworn she'd seen the same guy earlier, across the street from their house. She shook her head. Must be a coincidence. There were millions of people in London. Seeing the same person twice in one day was practically unheard of.

She continued down the street with Jed. The rain had stopped and the sun was making an attempt to shine. The meeting had gone well. It seemed that 'The Elphite' had made more at the box office than they had hoped for, which meant that she and Jed wouldn't have to worry about money for a while.

"Hey, Jed, how do you fancy going on a trip around the world?"

To read the alternate ending to The Elphite, visit michellegordon.co.uk/alternate-ending-elphite and join my mailing list to receive your free download!

About the Author

Michelle lives in England, in the middle of the woods. When not writing and publishing her own books, she helps other Indie Authors with their own publishing adventures. She has known all her life that she is a writer. It is more of a calling than simply a passion, and despite her attempts to live in the normal world, she has finally realised that she would much rather live in a world full of magic and mystery.

Please feel free to write a review of this book on Amazon, or even just click the Like button. Michelle loves to get direct feedback, so if you would like to contact her, please e-mail theamethystangel@hotmail.co.uk or keep up to date by following her blog – **eata.wordpress.com.** You can also follow her on Twitter **@themiraclemuse** or 'like' her page on Facebook.

To sign up to her mailing list, visit:
www.michellegordon.co.uk

The Earth Angel Series:

The Earth Angel Training Academy (book 1)

Velvet is an Old Soul, and the Head of the Earth Angel Training Academy on the Other Side. Her mission is to train and send Angels, Faeries, Merpeople and Starpeople to Earth to Awaken the humans.

The dramatic shift in consciousness on Earth means that the Golden Age is now a possibility. But it will only happen if the Twin Flames are reunited, and the Indigo, Crystal and Rainbow Children come to Earth, to spread their love, light and wisdom.

While dealing with all the many changes, Velvet struggles to see the bigger picture. When she is reunited with her Flame for the first time in many lifetimes, her determination and resolve to fulfil her mission falter...

The Earth Angel Awakening (book 2)

'No matter how overcast the sky, the stars continue to shine. We just have to be patient enough to wait for clouds to lift.'

Twenty-five years after leaving the Earth Angel Training Academy to be born on Earth as a human, Velvet (now known on Earth as Violet) is beginning to Awaken.

But when she repeatedly ignores her dreams and intuition, she misses the opportunity to be with her Twin Flame, Laguz. Without the long-awaited reunion with her Twin Flame, can Violet possibly Awaken fully, and help to bring the world into the elusive Golden Age?

The Other Side
(of The Earth Angel Training Academy)

Mikey is an ordinary boy who just happens to talk to the Faeries at the bottom of his garden. So when an Angel visits him in his dream and tells him he must return to the Earth Angel Training Academy in order to save the world, despite his fears, he understands and accepts the task.

Starlight is the Angel of Destiny. By carefully orchestrating events at the Academy and on Earth, she can make sure that everything works out the way that it should, even though it may not make sense to those around her.

Leon is a Faerie Seer. He arrives at the Academy as a trainee, but through his visions he realises that his role in the Awakening is far more important than he ever imagined.

The Visionary Collection:

Heaven dot com

When Christina goes into hospital for the final time, and knows that she is about to lose her battle with cancer, she asks her boyfriend, James, to help her deliver messages to her family and friends after she has gone.

She also asks him to do something for her, but she dies before he can make it happen, and he finds it difficult to forgive himself.

After her death, her messages are received by her loved ones, and the impact her words have will change their lives forever.

The Doorway to PAM

When Natalie is rejected by the one that she has loved for more than ten years, she finds herself lost, lonely and in the middle of the woods. It is here, in the most unlikely place, that she finds PAM's Tearooms. Within this unusual place, as well as a sweet, strong cup of tea, Natalie also finds her purpose and herself.

She discovers that a whole dimension exists, that is only ever found by souls in despair. Run by a lady called Evelyn, who is supported by dreaming volunteers, it is in this dimension that souls who are lost, find the meaning in their lives once more.

It is here, that Natalie finds the love that she has been yearning for.

I'm Here

When Marielle finds out that a guy she had a crush on in school has passed away, the strange occurrences of the previous week begin to make sense. She suspects that he is trying to give her a message from the other side, and so opens up to communicate with him, She has no idea that by doing so, she will be forming a bond so strong, that life as she knows it will forever be changed.

Nathan assumed that when he died, he would move on, and continue his spiritual journey. But instead he finds himself drawn to a girl that he once knew. The more he watches her, and gets to know her, he realises that he was drawn to her for a reason, and that once he knows what that is, he will be able to change his destiny.

In gratitude for the nourishing vibrational
energy of the trees that have sustained me for
so many years, I have created:

Sacred Tree Spirit

In this dream-like space, you can
receive intergrated therapies, emotional
and core-belief re-programming and
vibrational healing.
You can relax in the mineral spa,
watch life-affirming films in our
imaginarium, attend courses and shop
for handmade gifts.
Or you could just come along for a
drink and a cake to meet like-minded
people.

sacred-tree-spirit.com

Peace of Stone

9 Swan Court, Monmouth, NP25 3NY

Crystals

Jewellery

Gifts & Homeware

Crystal Therapy Treatments

Reiki Treatments

Hopi Ear Candling

Intuitive Workshops

www.peaceofstone.com

designs from a
different planet

madappledesigns
.co.uk

This book was published
by The Amethyst Angel.

A selection of books bought to publication by The Amethyst Angel.
To view more of our published books visit **theamethystangel.com**

We have a selection of publishing packages available or we can tailor a
package to suit each author's individual needs and budget. We also run
workshops for groups and individuals on 'How to publish' your own books.

For more information
on Independent publishing
packages and workshops offered
by The Amethyst Angel, please
visit **theamethystangel.com**

Printed in Great Britain
by Amazon.co.uk, Ltd.,
Marston Gate.